THE SHADOW OF SIN

Celesta was terrified. Parentless and alone save for the companionship of her old nurse, she had just learned that her brother Giles had lost their family home at the gambling tables. Celesta couldn't stay in her tiny cottage at the edge of the estate without the permission of the new owner, the Earl of Meltham.

But as soon as he saw his pretty new tenant, the Earl had other plans for her. He offered her his "protection," convinced that the destitute girl would jump at the chance to become a wealthy man's mistress. Celesta was horrified by the idea. But where could she turn for help to resist the Earl's unwanted advances?

BARBARA CARTLAND

Bantam Books by Barbara Cartland
Ask your bookseller for the books you have missed

THE SHADOW OF SIN

Barbara Cartland

BANTAM BOOKS · TORONTO · NEW YORK · LONDON

THE SHADOW OF SIN
A Bantam Book / June 1975
2nd printing
3rd printing

Published simultaneously in the United States and Canada

*Bantam Books are published by Bantam Books, Inc. Its trade-
mark, consisting of the words "Bantam Books" and the por-
trayal of a bantam, is registered in the United States Patent
Office and in other countries. Marca Registrada. Bantam
Books, Inc., 666 Fifth Avenue, New York, New York 10019.*

PRINTED IN THE UNITED STATES OF AMERICA

AUTHOR'S NOTE

The description of the Coronation of George IV, His Majesty's clothes, and the Banquet are all authentic. Queen Caroline died on August 8th, exactly twenty-one days after she was refused entry to the Abbey.

On the day of the Queen's death, the yacht *Royal George* had arrived off Holyhead. The King had all the masts of the squadron lowered as a sign of mourning. On August 12th, His Majesty's fifty-ninth birthday, he crossed the Irish Sea "in great spirits." The State Visit, the first few days of which the King remained quietly "in seclusion" as a mark of respect to his wife, was a triumphant success.

"The King was always fond of children," Lord Melbourne told Queen Victoria.

His Majesty bought an enormous amount of children's playthings to give away as presents. His accounts in the Royal Archives show bills for dolls and lead soldiers, boxes of ninepins, miniature farm yards, play houses, mechanical animals, rocking horses, games and toys of every description.

Chapter One
1821

Celesta, picking the peaches, was humming to herself.

The sunshine coming through the peach-house which had been built against one of the old red-brick Elizabethan walls shone on her fair hair and turned it gold.

The peaches were small because they had not been thinned in the Spring.

Celesta could remember when four peaches with one on top would fill the beautiful Sèvres dessert dishes which they had always used at the Priory.

Her father with a gold dessert knife would peel the rosy velvet skin from a peach and as he did so would say:

"I suppose all the large ones are being kept for the Show?"

"Of course they are!" her mother would say from the other end of the table. "You know that it would break old Bloss's heart if he did not win a prize."

It was a conversation which was repeated every year until her mother was no longer there. . . .

Celesta pulled herself together with a little jerk.

She would not think of that.

Instead as she picked the small but deliciously sweet peaches and placed them carefully in her basket she decided to whom she would give them.

There would be Mrs. Oakes, aged seventy-eight and crippled with arthritis, who would be delighted to have six, and little Billy Ives, who had broken his leg two weeks ago, should have another half a dozen.

And old Bloss's wife, who lived in a Cottage at the end of the village, would not only be thrilled to have the peaches but also the chance of a talk.

She had been very lonely since her husband had died.

And the rest, Celesta thought, when she and Nana had eaten as many as they could manage would be made into the delicious peach jam which was Nana's speciality.

Unfortunately they still had a few pots left over from last year, but it would be a pity to let the fruit go to waste.

She reached a little higher to where above her head there were three almost over-ripe peaches, and as she did so a deep voice from the broken doorway said:

"A very pretty thief, but nevertheless a thief!"

Celesta turned round in astonishment.

Standing just inside the peach-house was the most elegant Gentleman she had ever seen in her life!

Dressed in the very height of fashion with a high cravat and smart cut-away coat over tightly fitting champagne-coloured pantaloons, he seemed almost over-poweringly big in the low-roofed peach-house.

He was carrying his tall hat in his hand, his hair, cut in the wind-swept manner made fashionable by the King when he was Regent, was dark, and his eyes, strangely penetrating, seemed dark too.

Never, Celesta thought, had she seen a man who looked so handsome, so raffish and at the same time so cynical.

She was surprised into silence and the stranger with a mocking note in his voice continued:

"You must admit that I have caught you red-handed, but it would be a pity if someone as attractive as you should be prosecuted for crime."

He paused and his eyes seemed to flicker over Celesta's white skin, her deep blue eyes seeming too large for her small heart-shaped face, her tiny straight nose and sweetly curved red lips, before he went on:

"You can of course be hanged for stealing over five shillings worth of goods and if you escape the hangman, you still might be transported to New South Wales, a very unsavoury fate for such an alluring young woman!"

"Who . . . who are . . . you?" Celesta tried to say, but before she could enunciate the words he went on:

"On reflection I think it would be kinder if I were to be my own Judge and Jury. I therefore sentence you, my entrancing little intruder, to pay for the fruit you have so shamelessly taken from me."

"Who a-are you? What are y-you saying?" Celesta stammered.

"I think those are the questions I should be asking you," the stranger said.

He took a step nearer to her and then, almost before she could realise what was happening, before she could cry out or move, he put one arm round her and with his other hand lifted her face up to his.

She had one convulsive moment of fear as his lips came down on hers; then when she should have struggled and fought against him to be free she was unable to do so.

Celesta had never been kissed before and she did not know that a man's lips could hold a woman completely captive.

She was only conscious that his arm round her was strong and that his mouth, firm and demanding, was something beyond comprehension, beyond thought.

Her lips were very soft beneath his, and for a moment his arm round her tightened and the pressure of his mouth became more insistent.

Then as unexpectedly as he had taken her he set her free.

She made an inarticulate little sound which should have been a cry of fear but which died away in her throat.

Then, as her eyes met his, she stood for a moment spellbound before she turned and ran away.

She picked up the skirts of her cotton dress and
ran with a swiftness that had something of panic in
it through an opening in the walls.

It led from the lower garden into the upper one
and Celesta ran on past the gooseberry bushes and
the raspberry canes and through the gate which led
into the shrubbery.

Still running, she passed through the high rhododendron bushes which only a month before had been
a blaze of glory, then down the small path which led
to the Garden Cottage.

She pulled open the door and shut it behind her
to stand with her back against it breathing quickly
and feeling that she had shut out something which
menaced her.

"Is that you, dearie?"

It was Nana calling from the kitchen and her warm,
calm voice was somehow consoling.

"Y-yes!" Celesta managed to say a little unsteadily.

"Luncheon will be ready in a few minutes."

"I will go and . . . wash."

Celesta spoke automatically and as if in a dream
she walked slowly up the narrow oak staircase to
her bed-room on the floor above.

It was a small room and the diamond-paned window was open, so that there was the scent of the
roses climbing up the house and the sweet fragrance
of honeysuckle.

Celesta sat down on a stool in front of the dressing-
table and stared at herself in the mirror.

"How could it have happened?"

How was it possible she should have been kissed by
a complete stranger and done nothing to prevent it?

Then as she looked at her reflection in the mirror
she realised that he had of course mistaken her for a
girl from the village.

It was not surprising since with her fair hair un-
covered and blown by the summer breeze she had
been working in the garden all morning.

She was wearing a very old cotton dress which

had shrunk and faded from frequent washing. No lady could be expected to look like that or even be found unaccompanied in a garden as vast as the seven acres of vegetable gardens which were part of the Priory grounds.

Nevertheless, she told herself, he had no right, no right at all!

At the same time some part of her mind was saying: "So that is what a kiss is like!"

She had no idea that a man could seem so strong, so over-powering, or that his mouth could be so possessive. Then as she thought of it Celesta tried to be angry.

"How dare he?" she wanted to storm, but her anger turned only to shame.

How could she have been so weak, so spineless as to stand there and let it happen?

He was not really to blame. Men, she had always been told, did behave like that!

But for a lady to submit to such an intimacy without screaming, without attempting to fight against her assailant, showed a very reprehensible character.

Who was he and what was he doing there?

There seemed to be so many questions with no answers to what had occurred, and finally having washed her hands in the china basin which stood on the washing-stand, Celesta tidied her hair and went downstairs.

The table was laid for her in the small Dining-Room which until she and Nana had gone to live in the Garden Cottage had only been a large store-room attached to the kitchen.

Now furnished with a sideboard, a small walnut table, and four velvet-seated chairs it looked very elegant.

"Do we really need a Dining-Room?" Celesta had asked Nana when they had moved to the Garden Cottage.

"I'm not having you eating in the kitchen, Miss Celesta," Nana had said firmly. "We may be poor—

poverty-stricken some would say—but you'll behave like a lady as long as I'm with you, and that indeed is what your father would have wished."

"I only thought it would make more work for you," Celesta said quietly.

"You're a lady, bred and born, and you'll behave like one and there's no arguing against that!"

Now as Celesta seated herself so that she could look out of the small window onto the garden which she and Nana had made at the back of the Cottage she realised that something was wrong.

"What has happened, Nana?" she asked.

She was too close to her old Nurse, who had looked after her since she was a child, not to be aware of every mood, every changing intonation of her voice, and the tell-tale frown which appeared between her kindly eyes whenever she was worried.

"Eat your luncheon!" Nana said gruffly.

Celesta knew that this meant that something was really wrong.

Nana had a theory that no-one should eat when they were upset because it caused indigestion.

When Celesta was a child Nana would never scold her at meal-times or tell her anything that was unpleasant before she went to bed.

The dish set down in front of her while very simple was well-cooked and there were fresh vegetables from the garden which Celesta had herself brought into the Cottage earlier in the morning.

"Tell me, Nana!" she coaxed.

"You eat what I've put before you," Nana answered. "There's plenty of time for worrying after it's inside."

She went from the room as she spoke and Celesta smiled as she helped herself from a silver dish onto a plate of Crown Derby china.

So many treasures from the Priory had been brought to the Garden Cottage, but as Nana said:

"What's the point of leaving them for the rats and mice? Master Giles appears to have no interest in them, and it's nice for you to have your father's belongings round you."

"If Giles wants them I can always give them back," Celesta had said, feeling it salved her conscience.

At the same time when Giles told her that she and Nana must move from the Priory because he could no longer afford to pay the servants, she had naturally assumed that she would have to furnish the Cottage where old Bloss had lived for so many years.

Nana had complained more than Celesta.

"It's going down in the world to live like a labourer," she said, "and what your father'd say I can't imagine!"

'If Papa had lived it would never have happened,' Celesta thought.

Who could possibly have imagined that Giles, because he had succeeded to the Baronetcy and the small fortune their father had possessed, would have gone completely crazy?

It was all due, Celesta thought, to a man called Lord Crawthorne.

Looking back she could remember when Giles had first talked about him.

Her brother had come home that week with a number of his new gay London friends and the household had been rushed off its feet to offer them the sort of hospitality Giles had required.

He had developed very grand ideas since he had been to London, Celesta found. To begin with, he wanted far more footmen than poor old Bateson, who was on his last legs, could possibly produce or manage.

However, he brought some flunkeys down from London and very tiresome they were, treating the Priory servants with supercilious scorn and drinking far more ale than Nana thought was necessary.

Before his guests arrived Giles had talked to Celesta.

It was over a year ago and she was not quite seventeen. She learnt there was no question of her joining the party that evening or appearing at any other meals.

"You are too young," Giles explained. "Besides, it is going to be a very sophisticated party—the sort His Lordship enjoys."

"Who is this new friend of yours?" Celesta asked.

"Well, he is not exactly a friend," Giles said with a grin, "except that I like to think so. He is much older than I and very important. I cannot tell you, Celesta, how kind he has been to me."

"In what way?" Celesta asked.

"Well, he has shown me the ropes, introduced me to all the right Clubs, and taught me how to gamble, for that matter."

"Gamble?"

"You do not suppose I am going to lead a life like Papa's, do you?" Giles asked. "For one thing this Estate is not big enough to keep a man occupied, and anyway I have no use for the country when I might be in London."

"But, Giles, you have always been so fond of the country," Celesta protested. "You always said you would rather have a good day's hunting than go to a hundred parties!"

"That was before I knew what parties—real parties —were like!" Giles said with an almost ecstatic expression on his face. "You should see some of the places I have been to with His Lordship!"

Then he laughed.

"No, you should not. It is the last thing you should see! But I can tell you, Celesta, I felt a real green-horn when I first arrived in London. Now I am becoming what they call a very Tulip of Fashion!"

"Does that make you happy?" Celesta asked.

"It makes me enjoy myself," Giles answered. "I only wish to God I had more money! That is the only snag."

For a moment he was silent and then he said:

"My luck must change and when it does . . ."

"Oh, Giles, do be careful!" Celesta begged, but

even as she spoke she knew he was not listening to her.

She had peeped at the party through the banisters when they arrived in the oak-panelled Hall, and she watched them for a little while from behind the oak screen in the Minstrels' Gallery while they were at dinner.

They had sat down thirty that night and never had Celesta imagined women could be so alluringly beautiful or wear such décolleté evening-gowns.

She blushed when she realised how revealing the gowns were. Then she told herself that high above them in the Minstrels' Gallery was not the right way to judge their appearance, but at ground level.

As course succeeded course and the wine Giles had brought from London flowed very freely, it seemed to her that the party was growing very noisy.

Then Nana had dragged her away from the Gallery.

"It's not a sight I want you to see, Miss Celesta," she said. "Master Giles should be ashamed of himself bringing women like that to his home!"

"What is wrong with them?" Celesta asked.

But Nana had only pressed her lips together and looked so disapproving that Celesta had been awed into silence.

She had not seen Lord Crawthorne because Giles had seated him at the end of the table so that he had his back to Celesta peeping down from the Minstrels' Gallery.

She did notice, however, that his hair was growing a little thin on top and even at that distance she could see there were threads of grey amongst the neatly arranged curls.

She had hoped she might get a sight of His Lordship the following day, but he had left early, not, Giles hastened to add, because he had not enjoyed himself, but because he had a horse running at Epsom and wished to attend the Meeting.

The rest of the party had stayed on until, before

Celesta had expected them to do so, they all returned
to London.

"When will you be coming back, Giles?" she asked
her brother.

"When I have nowhere better to go," he replied.
"I am going to Newmarket next week to stay with
Hubert and the week after that to York where Freddie
has tremendous plans to amuse us."

"I am glad you are enjoying yourself," Celesta said
with all sincerity.

"I have never had so much fun in my life!" Giles
declared. "It is only . . ."

He stopped.

"It is only what?" Celesta asked.

"So damned expensive!" he answered. "But His
Lordship tells me that fortune favours the brave and
I believe him."

Celesta had not seen Giles again for six months.
Then he had come down to the Priory, removed nearly all the pictures, and told her he was shutting up
the house.

"How you can spend so much money I do not
know!" he exclaimed angrily when she had shown
him the house-keeping bills.

"We got rid of all the young servants when you
wrote to us three months ago," Celesta said, her eyes
worried. "You cannot turn off old Bateson and Mrs.
Hopkins. They have both been with us for over
forty years."

"I am not a Charitable Institution," Giles snarled.

Celesta looked at him in consternation. He seemed
to have altered in the last year.

His features had sharpened and there was something almost unpleasant about his eyes and the line of
his mouth.

"Are you very hard-up, Giles?" she asked with
some perception.

"I am practically below hatches," he snapped. "However the pictures ought to bring in something."

"You are selling them?"

"Of course I am! I have to get some money from somewhere."

"But, Giles . . . they are a part of our history . . . Papa always said so. They have been handed down from father to son for generations. You cannot sell them!"

"For God's sake stop nagging, Celesta," Giles shouted. "I have enough worries without you nattering on about some mouldy old canvasses that have been hanging on the walls where no-one ever notices them. I want money, I tell you. I want to enjoy myself! Is there nothing else in this dump I can sell?"

He had walked round the house, looking into every room and disparaging everything he saw.

The Priory was beautiful—to Celesta the most beautiful building in the world—but her father had left it very much as he had inherited it, and the furniture was ancient but not particularly valuable.

The Jacobean chests-of-drawers, refectory tables, and carved oak chairs, were all in perfect keeping with the ancient mullioned windows, the oak panelling, and the plasterwork on the ceilings, but they were not of fine enough workmanship to be worth much.

The velvet curtains, damask-covered chairs, and carved four-posters would, Celesta knew, fetch very little money away from the back-ground into which they blended so harmoniously.

In the end Giles had departed with the pictures and a few gold ornaments which Celesta could remember her father and mother using on very special occasions.

He also took the silver dishes made in the reign of Charles II which bore the Wroxley coat of arms. They were seldom used because there had not been enough servants to clean them.

Giles had also given specific instructions before he left: the gardeners were to be dismissed, old Bloss was to retire to a small Cottage at the end of the village.

Mrs. Hopkins and Bateson were given small pensions, and Celesta and Nana were to move into the Garden Cottage.

Since that time Celesta had not heard from him again.

She fortunately had a minute income of her own.

Her grandmother on her death had left a small sum to both her grandchildren and Celesta's share brought her in approximately fifty pounds a year.

It was just enough for her and Nana to live on, if they were not extravagant, as they did not have to pay rent. But it left very little for luxuries such as gowns, hats, shoes, and other clothes.

"Fortunately I need very little," Celesta said.

It was Nana who minded more that she was not fashionably dressed.

"For whom should I wear the latest fashion?" Celesta asked.

And for once Nana had no ready answer to that question.

As she finished her luncheon, Celesta wondered what could be upsetting Nana.

She had thought to tell her about the stranger who had behaved so badly in the peach-house, but then knew she could not explain her own reprehensible behaviour and therefore it would be better to say nothing.

Nana came back into the room.

"I've brought you a cup of coffee, Miss Celesta, and I thought you could have a peach to end the meal. Where did you put them?"

"I left them in the peach-house," Celesta said quickly. "I had not quite finished picking them."

"Oh well, you can have one for your supper," Nana said.

She put the cup of coffee down beside Celesta and then stood, her hands crossed over each other on her white apron.

"Now what is it, Nana?" Celesta asked gently.

"It's something Mr. Copple told me just half an

hour ago," Nana answered, "when he delivered the newspaper."

Celesta waited with a faint smile on her lips.

Mr. Copple, the village postman, was an inveterate gossip. There was nothing that went on in Wroxley village that he not only knew but was ready to repeat almost before it happened.

Although Nana said it was extravagant for Celesta to go on taking the *Morning Post* as her father had always done, it would have been a sad day if there had been no excuse for Mr. Copple to knock at the Cottage door.

"What dramatic crisis can have happened in the village?" Celesta asked as Nana did not speak.

"I can't believe it's true," Nana said, "but Mr. Copple says that a Nobleman with a whole carriage-load of servants has arrived at the Priory, and it's said that the Estate now belongs to him!"

"A Nobleman?" Celesta repeated in a very low voice. "Who is he? And how can he own the Priory?"

"Mr. Copple says," Nana answered, and her voice was low, "that Master Giles has lost it gaming."

"I do not believe it!"

Celesta rose to her feet as she spoke.

"It cannot be true! It cannot, Nana!"

"That's what I said, Miss Celesta, but there's no doubt that the Gentleman is there and Mr. Copple tells me there are more servants coming this afternoon."

Celesta put her hand up to her forehead.

She could not believe it, and yet something at the back of her mind told her that she had known all along that Giles would dispose of the Priory if he had nothing else left.

"How could he? How could he?" she whispered to herself.

The Priory in which the Wroxleys had lived for over five hundred years had always seemed to Celesta the most beautiful place in the world. It was her home and it was also Giles's.

How could he have thrown it away at the turn of
a card? How could he have thought so little of his
inheritance that having stripped the walls he had
now dispossessed himself of the Priory itself?

"There must be some mistake," she said aloud.

"I hope so . . . I very much hope so," Nana answered.

"What is the name of the gentleman who now
owns it?" Celesta asked.

She thought even as she spoke the words she knew
the answer.

"Mr. Copple was not certain," Nana answered, "but
he thinks . . ."

She was interrupted by a sudden loud rat-tat on
the front door.

The knocker was being applied forcefully—so
forcefully that the whole Cottage seemed to vibrate
to it.

"Now who could that be?" Nana asked. "If it's one
of them pestilential boys who knows that they should
come to the back door, I'll give him a piece of my
mind!"

She hurried from the Dining-Room and across the
tiny Hall. Celesta sat down in the chair she had just
vacated, her legs feeling curiously weak.

She knew she had already met the new owner of
the Priory, who, mistaking her for a labourer's daughter, had treated her with the familiarity her appearance had invited.

She could hear Nana speaking at the door. When
she came back to the Dining-Room she was holding
in her hand the basket of peaches which Celesta had
left in the peach-house.

"I don't understand it, Miss Celesta, and that's a
fact!"

"Who was that?" Celesta asked.

" 'Twas a groom from the Priory. He hands me the
peaches, says: 'His Lordship's compliments and he
hopes he may have the honour of calling on Miss
Celesta Wroxley at three o'clock this afternoon.' "

Celesta drew in her breath.

"No! No! I cannot see him!"

Her voice seemed to ring out in the tiny room and Nana looked at her in surprise.

"I don't understand, dearie, what His Lordship was doing with your peaches," she said, "but it's certain you must receive him, as I've told his groom."

"I cannot do that!" Celesta cried. "You do not understand, Nana. I cannot . . . meet him!"

"I don't know what's come over you," Nana said sharply as if Celesta were still five years old. "His Lordship is behaving in a very proper manner. It's only right that he should call on you. If it comes to that, it's the least he can do!"

"Did you ask his name?" Celesta asked in a weak voice.

"Of course!" Nana answered. "I know how to behave! 'May I ask, young man,' I says to the groom, 'the name of His Lordship? We've only just heard of his arrival at the Priory.'

"'My master's name,' he answered, 'is The Right Honourable the Earl of Meltham.'

"'Thank you,' I says, 'and will you inform His Lordship that Miss Celesta Wroxley will be pleased to receive His Lordship at the time suggested.'"

Celesta did not speak. She had been so certain that the new owner of the Priory would bear a different name.

Nana, accepting her silence as assent to what was suggested, went on reflectively:

"I'm thinking now that I've heard of His Lordship. Surely his name is often mentioned in that newspaper you read so carefully?"

"He is constantly in attendance on the King," Celesta said faintly.

"And one of the raffish Bucks that, as Regent, His Majesty was always entertaining at Carlton House, I shouldn't wonder!" Nana added.

"I think His Lordship is very distinguished and very wealthy," Celesta murmured. "Meltham House in Derbyshire is famous. I have seen pictures of it."

"Then what would he be wanting with the Priory?" Nana asked.

"That is what I do not understand."

Celesta paused for a moment and then the words seemed to burst from her.

"Oh, Nana! Nana! Do you really think it is true? Can Giles have lost the whole Estate at the gaming-tables? How could he do such a thing?"

"There's no accounting for what Master Giles will do these days," Nana said bitterly, and added in a low voice, "and he was such a dear little boy."

She walked from the room as she spoke and Celesta knew it was to hide her tears.

Nana had always loved Giles and given him an almost slavish devotion.

In consequence he had found her extremely ir-ritating.

"Keep that old woman away from me!" he would say to Celesta. "I am too old to be nannied!"

But Nana had gone on loving him. He had been "her baby" just as Celesta had been after she was born, but Giles had held first place in her heart.

'It was the same with Mama!' Celesta thought sometimes when she could bear to think of her mother.

Even when she was a very small child she had realised that when Mama came into the Nursery her face would light up as she lifted Giles into her arms.

It was Giles who always had the special tid-bit, the extra chocolate, the final good-night kiss. Yet he never seemed to want such affection as Celesta had wanted it.

Perhaps it was because he was a boy, or perhaps he was not a particularly loving person?

He had always been restless, he had always craved adventure, always wanted things to happen; while Celesta had been content with life as it was and the happiness of being at home.

Celesta stood in the Dining-Room for so long that

Nana with her eyes suspiciously red came back to see what was happening.

"Go upstairs and change, Miss Celesta," she said in her scolding voice which meant she was emotionally upset. "You'll find the new white muslin gown I made for you hanging in the wardrobe. Put it on, and for Heaven's sake do something with your hair. You look a real romp!"

"I do not suppose it will matter," Celesta said.

"It matters very much," Nana snapped. "I wish His Lordship to treat you with proper respect. After all, Miss Celesta, remember we are living on his property—he might wish to turn us off!"

"Turn us off?" Celesta's eyes were wide.

That was something she had not considered. But of course, if Giles had lost the Priory with its one thousand acres of land to the Earl of Meltham, the Garden Cottage would have gone too.

"He will let us stay. I am sure he will let us stay," she said in a voice that did not sound very convincing.

"Then make yourself pleasant," Nana told her. "I can't believe that any Gentleman would wish to turn you out of the only home you have, but then one never knows with these gamesters!"

She paused for a moment before she added:

"Make it very clear, dearie, that I'm not only in the position of being a servant but also your Chaperon!"

"My Chaperon?" Celesta repeated.

"That's what I said and that's what I meant," Nana answered. "You know as well as I do, Miss Celesta, that it's not right for a young lady of your age to live here alone without a Chaperon."

"Are you suggesting," Celesta asked with just a faint twinkle in her eyes, "that you should come into the Drawing-Room and sit with me while I receive His Lordship?"

"No, I wouldn't go as far as that," Nana answered, "but you can tell him that your father considered me

in the light of a Chaperon who could be trusted, and
that's what I am!"

Celesta tried not to laugh. Nana on her dignity
could be quite awe-inspiring.

At the same time she could not credit for a moment
that the Earl of Meltham would be in the slightest
degree concerned whether Miss Wroxley, who could
be mistaken for a village maiden, was conventional-
ly chaperoned or not.

But because she wished to show him how wrong he
had been in mistaking her identity, she took quite
an unusual amount of trouble over her appearance.

The muslin gown that Nana had made her was very
simple, but it was crisp and clean and the fact
that it was not in the fashion did not worry Celesta
unduly.

At last when she had arranged her fair hair
and clasped an enamel locket she had had since
a child round her neck, she looked very different
from the untidy wind-swept girl His Lordship had
surprised in the peach-house.

She was glad to see that the small Sitting-Room
which Nana sometimes called by the grand name of
Drawing-Room looked very attractive.

The sun was flooding in through the bow-window
which over-looked the small garden and at the other
end of the room there was a window onto the front
of the Cottage which stood back not far from the
road.

The bright chintz curtains seemed appropriate to
the ship's beams supporting the ceiling and the open,
brick fireplace in which reposed several large logs.

The sofa and chairs had all come from the Priory.
The pictures were small ones which Giles had not
thought worth selling, of the Wroxley family, mostly
of their children.

There were two vases of roses which Celesta had
arranged the previous day and which filled the room
with their fragrance.

And on the polished wooden floor there were rugs

which although worn still retained some of their
beautiful Persian colouring and intricate design.

It was a pretty room and a gracious back-ground
for a lady.

Celesta heard the sound of a carriage and horses
drawing up outside and the clock on the mantelpiece
showed it to be two minutes before three o'clock.

"His Lordship has come in style," she told herself.

She thought perhaps having discovered her identity
he was making a slight apology for what had taken
place that morning in the garden.

Then as she heard Nana open the door she found
unaccountably her heart was beating much quicker
than usual and she felt more shy than she had ever
felt in her life before.

She had a sudden impulse to run away, to refuse
to encounter again the man who had kissed her for
the first time in her life! A man who for some reason
she could not explain to herself had hypnotised her
into behaving in a very unaccountable manner.

Without meaning to do so she clasped her slim
fingers together as the door of the Sitting-Room
opened.

"The Earl of Meltham, Miss Celesta!" Nana announced impressively.

He came into the room and Celesta thought he
seemed even larger and more over-powering than he
had seemed in the peach-house.

She had not realised that his shoulders were so
broad or that he could move with a languid grace
which in itself seemed almost insufferably arrogant.

She had not forgotten the deep cynical lines on his
face, or that his eyes with the first penetrating glance
seemed to take in every detail of her appearance.

She swept him a deep curtsy, then found it hard to
look up.

"Your servant, Miss Wroxley."

She found it impossible to speak until with an
obvious effort she managed to say:

"Will you not sit down, My Lord?"

"Thank you."

He seated himself in a wing-back arm-chair which seemed particularly suitable for him.

He looked across the hearth to where Celesta had sat down on the very edge of a chair, forcing herself to look at him in what she hoped was an ordinary manner.

"I have only just learnt, Miss Wroxley, of your presence on the Estate," the Earl said. "Your brother somewhat unaccountably did not acquaint me with the fact."

"Is it true," Celesta asked in a breathlessly little voice, "that the Priory is now . . . yours?"

"I won it at cards from your brother two weeks ago," the Earl answered. "I gather he had little else to wager."

Celesta bit back the words which came to her lips. Then the Earl said in a kinder tone:

"It must have come as a shock to you; for I gather that until we met this morning you were not aware of what had occurred."

The colour rose in Celesta's cheeks.

"No, My Lord, I have not heard from my brother."

"Then it was undoubtedly a shock," the Earl said.

"How can you want the Priory?" Celesta asked without choosing her words. "You have your own house and from all I have read it is very grand. The Priory cannot be important to you."

"I think I might find it useful as it is so near London," the Earl answered. "Meltham, as you so rightly say, is a very grand residence and I am very proud of it. But it takes me two days to get there and as this is within driving distance of St. James's and on the road to Dover, it might at times prove a convenience."

Celesta pressed her lips together to prevent herself crying out at the lazy indifference in his voice.

'It means nothing to him,' she thought. 'Nothing at all that he should break a tradition and inheritance that had been in existence for five hundred years.'

There was a silence and then at length she said: "Do you wish me to . . . leave?"

"I think you must explain to me your exact circumstances," the Earl answered. "As I have already told you, Miss Wroxley, your brother did not inform me that you were living here in what I understand is called the Garden Cottage, or indeed that you were dependent upon him, if you are."

"My circumstances can be of little interest to Your Lordship," Celesta replied proudly.

"On the contrary," he replied, "as I understand your brother had very little, if any, money left, I must, if I have any sense of responsibility, find out how you are situated."

"My Nurse and I have enough to live on," Celesta said in a low voice.

"Exactly how much?" the Earl enquired.

"Can that really concern you?" Celesta asked almost indistinctly.

"Perhaps I am merely assessing how much rent you can afford to pay," he answered.

Celesta met his eyes and realised that for some reason of his own he was determined for her to tell the truth and there was nothing she could do but comply.

"My grandmother," she said quietly, "left me a small sum which brings in approximately fifty pounds a year."

"Is that all you have?"

"It is enough."

"It would not be enough for most young women of your age and with your looks!"

"Perhaps I am exceptional, My Lord."

"You must be," he said tartly, "unless of course you have planned for an early marriage. Are you engaged?"

"No!"

"But you have a number of Beaux who are pressing you to make up your mind?"

"There is no-one like that."

His lips curved in a smile.

"You can hardly expect me to believe such a statement."

"You can believe it because it is true!"

"What has happened to all the Gentlemen in Kent —are they blind?"

Celesta did not answer and after a moment he said:

"Why are you living like this, alone with your Nurse? Surely you are in need of chaperonage and there are friends with whom you could stay?"

"Nana is very insistent that she is an extremely proper Chaperon."

"I hardly think that your Nurse's contention would stand up to a social scrutiny," the Earl said. "So please answer my question. Is there no-one with whom you could stay?"

"No! No-one!"

"Why?"

"I think, My Lord, that is entirely my business."

"Come, Miss Wroxley. As I have already said, I have a sense of responsibility towards you. You are living here on my Estate and from what you have told me, you cannot afford to leave."

He paused to say slowly:

"I cannot believe that you are so innocent as not to realise there must be a certain amount of gossip, to say the very least of it, if you continue living at the Garden Cottage while I am at the Priory!"

Celesta looked at him wide-eyed for a moment, and then the colour crept up her cheeks.

"You ... you mean ..."

". . . exactly what you think I mean," the Earl finished.

"But it is absurd!" Celesta exclaimed and she rose to her feet.

Without realising what she was doing she walked across the room to stand at the bow-window looking out into the garden.

"You need not perturb yourself, My Lord," she

said. "I can assure you no-one in this part of the
world will be surprised at anything I do . . . if they so
much as give it a thought!"

There was a bitterness in her voice which was
very obvious.

After a moment the Earl said:

"I think you will have to explain that statement
to me."

"There is no reason for me to do so," Celesta replied.

Then she turned to look at him.

"Please, My Lord, let Nana and me stay here! We
will be no trouble and indeed there is no reason for
you to remember our very existence. I admit I have
no-where to go and I could not afford to pay rent
elsewhere. So please, because you have so much, be
. . . generous."

There was a break in Celesta's voice but the expression on the Earl's face did not alter.

His eyes were on her pleading eyes and on the
movement of her lips.

Then he said:

"I may do what you ask of me, but naturally I
wish first to know the full circumstances."

Celesta turned away again.

"If I do not tell you, there are plenty of people
who will!" she said. "Four years ago my . . . mother
ran away with a . . . neighbour!"

The Earl raised his eye-brows. It was obviously
something he had not expected to be told.

"May I know the neighbour's name?" he asked.

"The . . . Marquis of Heron," Celesta replied with
her back to him.

"Good Lord! And your mother's name is Elaine?"

"Yes."

"Then of course I have met her, but I had no
idea that this was where she had lived or indeed
that she had a daughter!"

Celesta did not speak and after a moment he went
on:

"So local Society has ostracised you because of your mother!"

"But of course," Celesta answered in a hard little voice. "Can you not realise that I might contaminate the girls of my age or entice their brothers into nameless indiscretions?"

"So I am to understand," the Earl asked, "that you are being made to suffer for something that is no fault of yours?"

"Nana has always said," Celesta replied, " 'Sin casts a long shadow.' "

Chapter Two

"Your mother is very lovely," the Earl said after a moment's pause.

As Celesta did not speak he went on:

"I remember the gossip when she ran away with the Marquis of Heron. They were, and still are, very much in love."

"We . . . loved her . . . too," Celesta said.

The words seemed to be forced from her and there was a pain in them that was unmistakable.

"I can understand that," the Earl remarked, "but I think your mother, like many women before her, felt the whole world was well lost for the man she loved."

Still Celesta did not speak and after a moment he said:

"One day when you fall in love yourself, you will understand."

"That is something I shall never do!" Celesta's voice was sharp.

She walked back to the hearth to sit down opposite the Earl.

"That is one of the reasons," she said in a carefully controlled voice, "why I am begging Your Lordship to allow me to stay here with my Nurse."

"For the rest of your life?" the Earl asked with a smile that she felt had something of mockery in it.

"For the rest of my life!" Celesta said firmly.

"You cannot be serious!" the Earl exclaimed. "Surely when you realise this is only a temporary unhappiness—if that is what you call it—you will marry

someone whom you love and will undoubtedly make
him an admirable wife."

"There is no reason why I should argue with
Your Lordship," Celesta said, "but I assure you that
I will never marry and I will never fall in love!"

There was something passionate in her voice and
the expression in her eyes was hard.

"I am sure you are far too intelligent to say anything which time will later disprove," the Earl replied.

Celesta made a little gesture of impatience and he
went on:

"I can understand it was hard for you as a child
to understand your mother's motives in creating a
scandal and leaving your father. But as an outsider
I can quite see there must have been extenuating
circumstances."

"You need not explain them to me!" Celesta said
firmly.

"Perhaps I am anxious to explain them to myself,"
the Earl said loftily. "For instance I have known the
Marquis of Heron since I was a boy although he is
older than I am. He has, as you very likely know, a
wife who is incurably insane. That is the reason why
your mother and he have not been able to marry
following your father's death."

Celesta turned her face towards the empty hearth
as if she did not wish to hear what was being said.

The Earl continued relentlessly:

"I believe there was a wide difference between
the ages of your father and mother. How old was
your father when he died?"

"He was . . . sixty-seven," Celesta answered reluctantly.

"One should never ask a lady's age," the Earl said
with a faint twist of his lips, "but I am sure I will
not be far out in my calculations if I presume that
your father was at least twenty-five years older than
your mother."

"They were married and they were happy!"

Celesta spoke almost like a child who has been goaded into an argument.

"Happiness does not always mean that two people are passionately in love," the Earl said, "and love, let me tell you, is for some people both a rapture and an over-whelming force which is irresistible."

"You are making excuses for Mama," Celesta said. "I do not know why you should do so unless you are prepared to condone the behaviour of the man who enticed her away from her home."

"I can understand that you miss her," the Earl said gently.

"I do not miss her now," Celesta replied, "but I want you to understand that I will never allow myself to be inveigled into behaving as Mama behaved, making other people unhappy, and allowing outsiders to sneer and laugh at me."

She spoke vehemently, then looked across the hearth at the Earl and finished:

"That is why I want Your Lordship to believe me when I say that, if you allow me to stay here on your property, it will be for life!"

"Under the circumstances it appears I have little alternative," the Earl said.

"Then Nana and I may stay?"

"If it pleases you."

He rose to his feet.

"As you know already, I never give without wishing to take. Therefore in return for my assurance that you may remain at the Garden Cottage, I ask one favour."

He saw Celesta's eyes widen a little apprehensively.

He waited a moment as if he wished her to be a little fearful before he went on:

"It is simply that you dine with me tonight."

"Dine with . . . you?" Celesta questioned.

"There is a great deal of history about the Priory which I would wish to know. I feel you are the right person to recount to me the legends of the past

and to tell me the whereabouts of the secret passages
and Priests' holes, of which I believe there are quite
a number."

"How should you know there are any?" Celesta
asked.

"Because I have already been told that they are
known only to each successive owner of the Priory
and his immediate family."

"There have been Wroxleys at the Priory for the
last five hundred years," Celesta said proudly.

"And now it belongs to me!" the Earl retorted.

"To you it is only a play-thing . . . a place where
you can stay because it is convenient. It means nothing! It is not and never will be your . . . home!"

Even as she spoke Celesta felt that she sounded
rude.

The Earl merely appeared amused, but he struck
back.

"First you hate your mother, and now you hate
me! And yet I think with a face like yours and
with such soft, sweet lips, you were made for love!"

He saw the anger in Celesta's eyes and the colour
which came into her cheeks, but before she could
speak he turned towards the door.

"I will send a carriage for you at seven o'clock," he
said and went from the room with the same lazy grace
and air of languor with which he had entered it.

He found Nurse waiting in the Hall.

"I shall expect Miss Celesta to dine with me this
evening," he said. "It is important that I talk to her
on various matters appertaining to her future."

"I'll see she's ready, M'Lord," Nana said.

She shut the front door behind him and went back
into the Sitting-Room.

Celesta was standing at the window looking out
into the garden, her hands clenched.

"I hate him, Nana!" she said, "I hate him, and yet we
have to be beholden to him."

"He will let us stay?"

"He says so, but he is insufferably arrogant, overbearing, and domineering! He has no right to speak to me as he has!"

"What has he said to you?" Nana asked quickly.

"He tried to excuse Mama."

She did not see the relief on the old Nurse's face.

"Why did you talk to him about Her Ladyship?" Nana asked after a moment. "You know it always upsets you."

"He said she is ... still very ... happy."

"And why not indeed?" Nana asked. "His Lordship was a fine Gentleman, even if what he did was wrong and a sin against the Commandments."

"Are you also excusing her?" Celesta asked. "Oh, Nana, how can you?"

"I'm not making excuses for Her Ladyship," Nana said stoutly. "What she did was wicked—a grievous sin. But it will do no good for you to go tearing your heart out and that's a fact! What's done is done!"

Celesta drew a deep breath.

"The Earl made me tell him why I have no friends and why there was no-one with whom I could stay."

"Much better know the truth from the very beginning," Nana said in a practical voice. "If he wants to come and live in this bigotted neighbourhood, he'll soon find out that people look down their noses at the goings-on in London. Still, like as not they'll accept him because he's a man!"

"Just as after Mama ran away they accepted Giles," Celesta said. "I was the one who was not good enough to enter their homes."

There was no bitterness in her voice now as there had been when she had spoken to the Earl, but rather the pain of someone who had been hurt almost intolerably.

Even now, after four years, Celesta remembered all too vividly how bewildered and stunned she had been when the friends she had known since childhood deliberately ostracised her.

Her father had been completely unaffected because he disliked Society anyway and had for some years refused all invitations.

He had been in ill health since he had had a riding accident when he was fifty.

It had affected the muscles in his back, and as the years went by he was almost continually in pain.

It made him at times querulous and disagreeable, and it also made him dislike having to entertain or be entertained.

They had therefore lived a very quiet life at the Priory, but Celesta had realised that her mother made a great effort where she and Giles were concerned to see that they had companions of their own age.

She remembered children's parties to which they had driven miles. There had been parties too at the Priory, with picnics in the summer and games and dancing in the winter.

Now the Earl's remark about the disparity between the ages of her parents made her realise as if for the first time that her mother might have found such an existence dull.

The only interest Lady Wroxley had besides looking after her husband and children was that she loved riding.

Sometimes she would go hunting in the winter, but at all times of the year there was seldom a day when she did not ride in the morning for perhaps two hours and return, her face glowing with the exercise, a sparkle in her eyes.

At first she had always been accompanied by a groom, but then she acquired a horse that was too fast and too spirited for anything else in the stable to keep up with it.

"I do think you ought to take Hickman!" Celesta heard her father remark once.

It was when her mother had come home to say she had fallen at a fence but had managed to catch her horse again and remount.

"Hickman is getting old," Lady Wroxley had replied with a laugh, "and you know that Merlin can out-ride, out-jump, and out-pace any of those old cart-horses you have in the stables!"

"I am not buying any more horses," Sir Norman said sharply.

"Then I must ride alone," his wife replied.

She had laughed lightly and then bent down to kiss his cheek.

"Do not worry about me," she pleaded. "I promise you I am quite capable of looking after myself."

The Priory Estate marched with that of the Marquis of Heron.

As Celesta grew older she heard whispers about the Marquis's wife and her strange and uncontrollable behaviour.

Then from the servants she learnt that the Marchioness of Heron had become completely insane and had been put in a private asylum.

"It is a real shame," she heard Nana say to the Head House-Maid. "A fine, upstanding man like that without even an heir to the title!"

"They say that lunatics live for ever!" the House-Maid had replied. "It's not right that those as is married to them can't get free."

"That's the law," Nana said, "and there's nothing anyone can do about it."

'If I had been older,' Celesta thought afterwards, 'I might have realised what was happening.'

But at fourteen she was not particularly observant and in a way young for her age.

An older person would have noticed that Lady Wroxley had never looked more beautiful.

There was a tenderness and a light in her face that had never been there before.

The daughter of an impoverished country Squire, she had been married off at seventeen to the first man who asked her.

Sir Norman Wroxley had arrived one autumn day to shoot with her father and she had gone out with

the guns, chattering animatedly to her father's guests
and in her mother's absence acting as Hostess at
luncheon.

She had seemed unbelievably lovely to the much
older man who had never been particularly interested
in women.

Sir Norman had not been married before simply
because he had never found anyone whom he wished
to make his wife.

In middle-age he suddenly fell deeply in love.

He was however far too set in his ways to change,
and he merely tried to absorb his young wife into
his very stereotyped life.

Elaine Wroxley had a warm affection for her husband, but when she met the Marquis of Heron she
was emotionally unawakened.

To both of them love was rapturous, wonderful,
and over-whelming. What happened was inevitable.

But it was impossible to explain that to a fourteen-
year-old girl when everything she had thought secure
collapsed about her.

"How could Mama do such a thing? How could
she?" Celesta had asked then, and she asked it again
now.

She remembered waiting for the invitations from
her friends which never came.

"Lady Selton is giving a dance for her daughter's
fifteenth birthday next month," Nana said soon after
Lady Wroxley had run away. "You'd best be getting
yourself a new gown."

"Yes, of course," Celesta had replied. "I wonder
Elizabeth has not ridden over to tell me about the
party. She was full of it when I last saw her."

She could remember waiting day after day for the
invitation which never came.

It was only the first of a dozen snubs and slights
before she finally understood that Kent Society would
no longer accept her.

Her father said very little. It seemed to Celesta

that without her mother he had decided it was not worth while going on living, so he died.

The Doctors told her this was nonsense.

"Your father has been in pain for years, and he undoubtedly had a growth due to his accident."

"It was a broken heart!" Celesta told herself.

But she was not quite certain whether it was her own heart or her father's which was most involved.

Giles had taken it all light-heartedly, but then Giles was not living at the Priory but had gone to London as soon as he came down from Oxford.

At first he was content with the company of his friends he had made at school and at college.

It was only after his father died and he inherited the title that he really began, as he said himself, to enjoy life.

'If Mama had been there he would not have been so wild!' Celesta thought. 'And he certainly would not have gambled away the Priory!'

And yet she could not be sure of that.

By the time he left Eton, Giles had begun to think of both his parents as old-fashioned and out-of-date.

When his mother had run away with the Marquis of Heron he had taken it calmly and philosophically; he merely said:

"I expect Mama got fed up with Papa carping at her."

Nana broke into Celesta's thoughts:

"Come along, Miss Celesta! Stop day-dreaming. It won't be long before you have to change and I'll heat the boiler so's you can have a bath. You had best wear your new gown. You might not get another chance!"

"No!" Celesta's voice was decisive. "I will not wear that! Never, Nana, do you understand? Never! Never!"

"Well, it seems a waste," Nana said. "I can try to copy the new style, but we couldn't afford material like that and it's a beautiful dress, it is really!"

"I have told you, Nana, that I am not wearing anything that Mama sends me! Never!"

Celesta hurried out of the Sitting-Room and into the garden.

Nana watched her go and then she sighed.

Ever since she had left, Lady Wroxley had sent presents from France for Celesta at Christmas and on her birthday.

There had been soft suede gloves which only the French could make; shifts of fine Chinese silk embroidered with real lace; day-dresses which, simple though they might be, had a Parisian chic about them.

Then this year at the beginning of the Summer there arrived a gown which had made Nana gasp as she opened the box.

Both she and Celesta had known quite well why it had come.

Lady Wroxley had thought that Celesta would be making her début at the age of eighteen and this was a Ball gown.

"I've never seen anything so lovely, dearie!" Nana had exclaimed as she drew it out of its box.

"I do not wish to look at it!" Celesta had cried. "I do not wish to see it!"

She had walked out of the house, leaving Nana standing with the gown in her hands and an understanding look in her old eyes.

It was obvious that Lady Wroxley had no idea that because of her scandalous behaviour her daughter was never asked to Balls, so there would be no possible occasion on which she could wear the gown which she had sent to her.

It was exquisitely lovely. Of white gauze over white satin, it was trimmed with row upon row of real Valencian lace round the hem, arranged in scallops and caught up with bunches of white camelias.

There was lace round the boat-shaped neck and camelias with velvet ribbon to decorate the small sleeves and the new tight waist.

Nana realised that Celesta would look outstandingly beautiful in it—but she would not even try it on.

The dress had been hung away in a cupboard where all the other gifts her mother had sent to her over the years were still in their boxes.

As usual, the sunshine and the scent of flowers, the soft murmur of the breeze in the trees calmed Celesta and swept away the feeling of anger, agitation, and resentment which had all been aroused in her by the visit of the Earl.

There was something about him, she told herself, that was very disturbing.

He had upset her by the manner in which he had behaved in the peach-house and it seemed now as if he had re-opened wounds which she had thought were healed when he talked of her mother.

She felt a deep reluctance to go to the Priory tonight and have dinner with him.

She was aware too that if they were, as she suspected, to be alone, it was in a way an insult that he should ask her to dine with him unchaperoned.

Then she told herself it was just what she might expect, having told him of the circumstances in which she found herself and being already an outcast from local Society.

"I am neither fish, fowl, nor good red herring," Celesta said aloud, quoting one of Nana's favourite sayings.

Nevertheless when she was finally ready and the carriage was waiting outside to carry her the short distance to the Priory, she looked lady-like and very lovely.

Nana had attempted to copy a gown that Lady Wroxley had sent from Paris two years earlier.

Pale green—the original had been of gauze but Nana could only afford muslin—it had the high waist that was now almost gone out of fashion, but it revealed the soft maturity of Celesta's breasts and the straight skirt could not hide the slender curves of her body.

The colour of the gown made her skin seem dazzlingly white, and her fair hair had been set off by
Nana with two white rose-buds which had been
picked from the garden.

"It is ridiculous sending me a carriage!" Celesta
said as if wanting to find fault. "It takes me three
minutes to walk across the garden to the Priory, instead of which we have to go up the road, in through
the main gates, and down the drive!"

"His Lordship would hardly expect his guests to
arrive on foot," Nana remarked.

"I imagine I will be the only guest there," Celesta
retorted.

She was right!

The Earl was waiting for her in the large Salon on
which her mother had indelibly imprinted her personality.

The blue damask curtains which framed the diamond-paned windows, the white panelled walls with
the cornices picked out in gold leaf, had been a fitting
back-ground for Lady Wroxley's beauty.

Yet it seemed to Celesta that the room also ad-
justed itself to the Earl, who stood at the far end of
it beside a marble mantel-shelf which had been carved
in Italy.

She had never imagined a man could look so elegant in his evening clothes.

Although she told herself she hated him, it was
impossible not to admire the intricate folds of his
high cravat, the superb fit of his evening coat, and
the elegance of the one black pearl stud which glittered in his pleated shirt front.

Despite the smartness of his clothes he wore them
with a casual air which somehow made them a part
of himself.

As she moved towards him, just for one fleeting
second Celesta regretted that she was not wearing the
gown which had arrived from Paris for the "coming-
out Ball" she never had.

Then she told herself all she had to do was to make

sure that the Earl was prepared to allow them to remain in the Garden Cottage, and the less she saw of him, the better!

She curtsied and as she rose he said quietly:

"I see now you are very much like your mother. When I first met her I thought she was one of the most beautiful women I had ever seen!"

"I have no wish to . . . talk about Mama!" Celesta said stiffly.

"I am determined to continue our conversation where it left off," the Earl said, "and I think you will find it difficult to prevent me from doing something I wish to do."

'That is true,' Celesta thought as she seated herself on the sofa.

There was a strength and determination about the Earl which she recognised even while she disliked him. There was something ruthless about him which made her feel young and unsure of herself, and she hated him the more because of it.

"Your home is very beautiful, Miss Wroxley," he said disarmingly.

The Butler, a very superior-looking man attended by two footmen, offered Celesta a glass of Madeira.

She accepted it, remembering as she did so that she had not tasted alcohol since her father's death.

The Earl preferred a dry sherry and as the servants withdrew he said:

"I have been over the house since I left you this morning, and there are a great many questions I want to ask you about it. I know of course it was originally a Cistercian Monastery, but I think only you will be able to tell me what has taken place here down the centuries."

"Then there are several books in the Library which should interest Your Lordship . . ." Celesta began.

By the time dinner was over she found that for the moment at any rate she had forgotten to hate the Earl.

She had thought that she was the only person interested in the battles which had taken place round the Priory; in the Priests who had hidden from Queen Mary's avenging Papists and then from Elizabeth's reforming Protestants, and who between them had created the Priests' holes and at one time used the small Chapel hidden in the rafters.

Later had come the Royalists fleeing from Cromwell's Armies, and once again the Priests' holes had proved invaluable to the fugitives who, if discovered, would have forfeited their lives.

The Earl, Celesta found, was a good listener.

She had no idea how her eyes shone and her face glowed, and her voice deepened with emotion as she told the story of her ancestors.

When dinner was over they left the Dining-Room with its fine Minstrels' Gallery and big baronial fireplace for the Library, where Celesta climbed up the twisting mahogany steps, which could be moved from one bookcase to another, to find the volumes she wanted the Earl to read.

She was coming down, having taken a book from a top shelf, when he stood at the bottom of the steps and did not move as she came level with him.

She had been talking so animatedly on a subject in which she was interested that it was now as if she remembered for the first time that he was a man and they were alone.

There was something in his eyes and in the faint smile on his lips that checked the words she had been about to speak.

"You are very lovely, Celesta!" he said in his deep voice.

She realised it was the first time he had used her Christian name.

"I . . . I want to tell you about this . . . book," she said quickly.

"The book can wait!" he answered, "I want to talk about you!"

"What about . . . me?"

It was impossible for her to move when she was still two steps up from the floor.

"I have been thinking about you."

"There was no need. You have been kind enough to say that Nana and I can stay at the Garden Cottage. When you go back to London, forget about us."

"Will you forget about me?"

"I hope so."

"Have you forgiven me for kissing you this morning?"

Celesta tried to prevent herself from blushing, but the question made her feel confused.

"I shall . . . try to forget . . . it," she said at length.

"But I shall not do so. It was enchanting! Something I want to remember!"

"You had no . . . right to behave as you . . . did, except that I looked so . . . untidy."

"You looked lovely—just as you look now! I had not expected to find anyone so beautiful hidden away in the country."

"Thank you," Celesta said, "but I do not think you . . . ought to speak to me like . . . this."

The Earl raised his eye-brows.

"Is it offensive to you?"

"Not exactly. But it is . . . embarrassing . . . I am not used to . . . compliments."

"Then I think it is time that you started to hear them."

"Why?"

"Because otherwise it would be a waste. A waste of youth and beauty and of course of love!"

"You know already what I think about . . . love!"

"Of which you know nothing!"

"For that I am glad!" Celesta said firmly.

For a moment the Earl did not reply and while Celesta waited, aware that her heart was beating rather quickly in her breast, and there was a strange feeling in her throat which she thought was fear, he walked abruptly away from her.

He crossed the Library to stand at the big desk in

the centre of the room at which her father had once
worked.

He looked down at the blotter ornamented with
the Wroxley Coat of Arms, the ink-pot engraved with
the Wroxley Crest, as was the ivory paper-opener encircled with bands of gold on which was a lion
rampant above a scroll bearing the words in Latin:
"Loyal to our Ideal."

"There are so many things I should say to you,
Celesta," the Earl said after a moment, and his voice
held a note in it she did not understand.

"About what?" she asked, descending the last two
steps to stand on the carpet looking at him a little
uncertainly.

"I have told you—about yourself," he said.

"What is wrong? What are you trying to say?"
Celesta asked.

She had a sudden fear that he had changed his
mind . . . that after all he wanted her to leave, and
wondered frantically where she and Nana could go.

"You are too beautiful to be living as you are,"
the Earl said. "Sooner or later someone will discover
you and then—God knows what could happen!"

"I do not understand," Celesta said. "What could
happen?"

"What I would like to do," the Earl went on as if
she had not spoken, "is to offer you my protection. I
would be very kind to you, Celesta—very gentle—
and I believe I could make you happy."

Celesta looked at him with a puzzled expression
in her eyes.

"I do not think I . . . understand," she said in a
confused tone.

Then suddenly, almost as if she had been struck
by lightning, she understood what he meant.

"Are you saying . . . can you mean . . . ?"

Her voice died away. The Earl turned and came
nearer to her.

"You said you had no wish to marry," he said. "Well
neither have I, but I can give you all the things in

life you are lacking and bring you so many delights that you do not even know exist."

"How . . . could you? How could you say such . . . things?" Celesta asked. "I suppose because of Mama you think I am like that too! That I would live with a man . . . be his mistress. That is what you are saying, are you not?"

"A harsh word for something that can be very lovely," the Earl answered, "and I promise you, Celesta, that I do not mean to insult you. It is just that there seems to be little alternative for either of us."

"I want only to be left alone!" Celesta said.

"That is what you think at the moment, but I promise you, my dear, that it is not only impractical but unlikely."

Celesta lifted her chin.

"I accept, My Lord, that you are not intending to insult me, although that is what it appears to be! But let me tell you that I would rather . . . die than accept your proposition!"

"I wonder if you will say the same thing in a year's time?" the Earl answered.

"One year, two years, ten years," Celesta replied, "my answer will be the same. It is no, My Lord! No! No! No!"

She thought he might argue with her.

Instead he merely smiled and she thought he was mocking her.

"Then let us talk of other things," he said. "I have no wish to upset you."

"You have already upset me," Celesta said almost challengingly. "Please, I would like to go home."

"And leave a barrier between us?" he asked. "A barrier that would undoubtedly grow brick by brick as you thought about it. No, Celesta, I want you to remember me in a very different manner, and so we will now continue our tour of the house."

Celesta wanted to refuse.

She wanted more than she had ever wanted anything in her life to run away from him; to escape from the feeling that, although he had not touched her, his arms were round her.

She had already felt his strength and she knew that the power that seemed to exude from him was stronger still.

He was willing her, commanding her, and she felt that however fast she might run, however hard she tried, she would never be able to escape him.

But because he almost forced her to do so, she made herself take him round the Priory and show him all he wished to be shown.

Only when they entered together a Priests' hole and he shut the door so that she could show him how to find the secret catch which would open the hidden panel did she feel a tremor of real fear because they were so close.

For a moment they were in darkness, yet she felt she could see him as clearly as if they were standing in the sunlight.

He was so big and over-powering and there were some strange vibrations from him which seemed to affect her both mentally and physically.

She thought he might put his arms round her, but he did not do so and when she found the secret catch he merely put his fingers over hers to feel where it was.

At the touch of his hand she felt a strange sensation which she could not explain to herself.

Then the panel swung open and they stepped into the room which was known as the Master-Bedchamber.

"As you see, I am sleeping here," the Earl said.

Celesta saw his gold brushes which stood on the dressing-table which her father had used and his satin robe was thrown over a velvet chair which stood in front of the fire.

"Remember," Celesta said, "if you should ever wish to escape you can go through the secret Priests' hole, down the twisting stairs, and the secret passage comes out beside the Chapel in the West Wing."

"It might prove useful—who knows?" the Earl said.

Then Celesta led the way into the other State Bed-rooms on the first floor.

"Which was your bed-room?" the Earl asked.

Celesta opened a door to a small room which was empty of furniture.

"I have taken everything that was here to the Cottage," she said.

Then her fingers went up to her lips as she spoke in a gesture of consternation.

"Perhaps I should have told you . . . before," she said, "that everything in the Cottage is . . . yours too. It all came from the Priory."

"I thought this afternoon how charming your room looked," the Earl said.

"If there is . . . anything you want back . . ." Celesta began.

"I am quite prepared to provide a roof over your head, a bed in which you can sleep, and a chair in which you can sit," he answered. "I would only wish that you were not quite so selfish about it."

"Selfish?" Celesta asked without thinking.

"That you will not share them with the man who actually owns them," the Earl said.

She turned away from him.

"I can only hope that you will not go on speaking of this, My Lord. I have given you my answer."

"Do you really think I will accept defeat so easily? I assure you, Celesta, that when I want something I am a relentless hunter and an indefatigable fighter."

Celesta was still and then she said:

"Please . . . please leave me alone. You . . . frighten me! And although I want to run away from you . . . I have no-where to . . . go!"

There was silence and then the Earl said in his mocking voice:

"I think you are extremely skilful in using what weapons you have at your command. Let me tell you, Celesta, that you have just won a minor battle!"

They went downstairs. When they reached the Hall the Earl said to the attendant flunkeys:

"The carriage for Miss Wroxley."

"It is waiting, My Lord."

Celesta's cloak was placed over her shoulders. She held out her hand to the Earl.

"Thank you ... My Lord," she said softly.

She knew he would understand that she was thanking him for more than her invitation to dinner.

"I am leaving tomorrow," he said as he raised her hand to his lips, "but I hope, Miss Wroxley, we shall meet again in the not too distant future."

Celesta curtsied, then walked away from him and out into the waiting carriage without looking back.

"Did you enjoy yourself?" Nana asked as soon as she arrived home. "Has His Lordship made any alterations? Who was there?"

Celesta put her cloak down on a chair.

Somehow she replied to Nana's questions. All she wanted was to be alone in her own bed-room, but it was some time before this could be achieved.

Nana hung up her dress, helped her into her nightgown, brushed her hair, and finally tucked her up in bed as she had done ever since she was a child.

"Good-night, my dearie," she said from the door. "I shall thank Almighty God tonight that you and I can stay on here. You know as well as I do there is no-where else we could go. Not with the little money we have to spend."

"No, Nana. I am glad we can stay."

"Good-night, dearie. Don't worry about anything— just go to sleep. I only hope I can do the same."

The door shut and at last Celesta was alone.

Lying in the darkness, she could hardly believe that so much that was disturbing and disruptive had taken place in the same day.

She could hardly believe even now that Giles had gambled away the Priory; that she and Nana could remain on in the Garden Cottage only by an act of charity on the part of the Earl of Meltham.

He had in fact offered her a very different dwelling-place.

"How could he imagine for a moment," she asked herself, "that I would accept such a proposition? How could he think I would become his mistress simply so that I could be more comfortable, and because, according to him, I need the protection of a man?"

There seemed no answer to her questions.

"I am perfectly safe here with Nana," she said aloud in the darkness.

Then she wondered whether the fact that the Earl was now at the Priory would not bring new dangers to her peaceful existence.

There might be men staying with him who if they found her in the Cottage would wish to kiss her, as he had done.

If they knew she was there it might be impossible for her to prevent them from calling. To stop them from making love to her as a man had made love to her mother?

Celesta felt herself tremble at the thought.

She had a horror of love.

It was something that was so unrestrained, so uncontrollable, that a woman could lose all sense of propriety and could throw away her whole past, her husband and children, merely for some new emotion she felt for a stranger.

If her mother could do that—her mother, who had always seemed so controlled, so level-headed, so sensible—could she too not be affected by the same emotions should the occasion arise?

Celesta drew in her breath.

If she loved the Earl, would she not have found it easy tonight, when he had suggested that he should protect and look after her, to say yes?

Supposing when they had been together in the Priests' hole he had put his arms around her and kissed her as he had done earlier in the day. What would she have done?

She had an uncomfortable feeling that once again

she would have been unable to scream or fight against him.

She had been hypnotised into accepting the touch of his lips, the manner in which they had held hers completely captive.

"I hate love! I hate it!" she told herself. "It is wrong! It is wicked! It can destroy everything that one believes in!"

And yet even as she whispered the words with a passionate intensity she found herself thinking how fascinating it had been to talk to the Earl about the history of the Wroxleys and know that he was listening to her attentively.

She had never before dined alone with a man and had not realised how easy it was to talk when one was not surrounded by a crowd of other people laughing and chattering.

She even felt that some of the things she had said were witty and she had found herself using words and sentences she hardly realised she knew.

She had described so clearly the battles that had taken place in the past and the apprehension of the fugitives as they had shivered in the Priests' holes, hearing the soldiers searching for them just the other side of the panelling.

'Mama always said I had a vivid imagination!' Celesta thought.

And then she found herself wondering what her mother had felt the first time the Marquis of Heron had kissed her.

How many times had they met, perhaps in one of the woods which bordered the Estates, before he had put his arms round her?

Had she felt it was impossible to move or protest as his lips touched hers?

"It was wrong! She should never have seen him again!" Celesta said aloud.

A kiss could lead to so many things and finally to a woman running away in the middle of the night as her mother had done, leaving only a note for her husband to read the following morning.

Then, before she could prevent it, Celesta found herself remembering how the Earl had excused her mother's actions.

"How old was your father when he died?" he had asked, and she could hear her own voice replying:

"Sixty-seven."

"Papa might have been twenty-five years older than Mama," Celesta told herself now, "but that was no excuse. She was his wife and our mother! She should have stayed with us!"

Then again she could hear the Earl saying:

"Love is an over-whelming force which is irresistible!"

Celesta moved in the darkness.

"I must never fall in love!" she told herself. "Never! Never!"

But even as she said the words a part of her mind was asking:

'I wonder what it would be like?'

Chapter Three

The Earl of Meltham drove down Piccadilly the following morning before eleven o'clock.

Wroxley Priory was less than two hours' drive from London and the Earl's fine horse-flesh travelled at a greater speed than could be achieved by ordinary horses.

He was proceeding to Carlton House, where he had an appointment with the King.

For months past carpenters and joiners, painters and upholsterers had been hard at work at Westminster Abbey and Westminster Hall, and the route from Carlton House to the Abbey was in the process of being decorated.

Tomorrow morning, the 19th of July, the Coronation of King George IV was to take place.

Amid the ostentatious grandeur of Carlton House, which the Earl thought was more packed with antique treasures and priceless works of art than a plum pudding, the King was waiting for him in the Eastern Glory of the Chinese Drawing-Room.

His face lit up when he saw the Earl.

"I heard you were out of London, Meltham," he said, "and I was afraid you might have forgotten we were meeting this morning."

"I have just returned from the country, Sire," the Earl replied, "and I assure you I was not likely to forget anything so important as the fact that you wished to see me."

"I want you to look at my Coronation robes," the

King said. "They were finished only yesterday, and you know I value your opinion."

He spoke with an eagerness which had something youthful about it and belied his fifty-ninth year.

He had, the Earl noticed, discarded the russet whiskers which until recently had bristled on his cheeks, giving his face a rather choleric, almost bucolic look.

Now he looked surprisingly young and the Earl knew it was because he was excited about his Coronation.

Every detail had been planned by the King himself and actually no-one could have done it better.

He led the way, walking quickly despite his weight, to an Ante-Room in which were arranged the Coronation robes he had designed and which the Earl had already heard had cost over £24,000.

The ermine alone accounted for £855 of this sum.

The King's crimson velvet train ornamented with golden stars was certainly astounding. It was twenty-seven feet long.

"I intend to wear with it," His Majesty said, "this hat."

He held it up as he spoke. It was a huge black Spanish hat surmounted by sprays of ostrich feathers and heron plumes.

"You will certainly look magnificent, Sire," the Earl said.

"The Privy Councillors are to wear blue and white satin Elizabethan costumes."

The Earl had already heard this from Lady Cowper, who had added spitefully:

"They will undoubtedly convulse the whole of Westminster Abbey with laughter!"

The Earl however knew that the King's taste, even if it was at times flamboyant, was always basically good, and though the Coronation robes looked extraordinary lying in the Ante-Room at Carlton House, he had the feeling that in their right setting they would be impressive.

"I have tried to think of everything," the King said almost pathetically.

"I am sure you need not worry, Sire," the Earl told him, "and indeed we are all looking forward to the ceremony even if it will be somewhat exhausting."

"I only hope everything goes smoothly," the King muttered almost beneath his breath.

The Earl glanced at him and understood his apprehension.

The trial the previous year in which the Queen had been brought before the House of Lords to answer a charge that her "scandalous, disgraceful, and vicious conduct" had made her unworthy of the title of Queen Consort had been a disaster.

It was true that no man in the King's position had ever suffered more from the way his wife had behaved in providing Europe with a scandalous amusement which delighted his enemies.

In Genoa she had been drawn through the streets in a gilt and mother-of-pearl phaeton.

At Baden she had appeared at the Opera in an enormous peasant's head-dress decorated with flying ribbons and glittering spangles.

In Genoa she attended a dance *en Venus,* naked to the waist, displaying, the King had been told, a bosom of more than ample proportions.

What was more, on the way to Constantinople she had spent her time in a tent on board the ship with her Italian Chamberlain, a lively young man six feet high with a magnificent head of black hair and moustachios of which an observer said, "they reached from here to London."

She made him "Grand Master of the Order of Caroline," which she had created in Jerusalem, and the King's spies produced the most disgusting and damaging reports of their behaviour both in public and private.

This was only some of the evidence which was brought before the House of Lords. Unfortunately it was mostly attested by servants and the Queen herself aroused the sympathy of the masses.

When she answered the accusations of adultery with the spirited reply, "I have only once committed adultery and that was with the husband of Mrs. Fitzherbert," the mob liked her courage and cheered her whenever she appeared.

After proceedings which had lasted almost three months, the Government had realised they would never get their Bill through the House of Commons and the charge was withdrawn.

For three nights flambeaux and lights were kept burning all over London and those who refused to express their joy had their windows smashed.

The King, an object of ridicule, had retired to Windsor lonely and depressed.

The Earl knew that the Queen had made the very most of her victory and was delighted with the publicity she had received.

"Her Gracious Majesty takes care to keep it up," Lady Sarah Lytleton told the Earl, "by showing herself all over London in a shabby post-chaise and a pair of post-horses and living in the scruffiest house she can think of to show she is kept out of the Palace."

Only the previous week Lord Temple had said:

"Fears of riots are making it difficult to sell stands along the Processional route."

There was no need for the King to say much.

He knew that the Earl, like all his closest friends, was deeply concerned as to what might happen on the day of the Coronation.

"Do you really think it will be all right, Meltham?" His Majesty asked now.

He was almost, the Earl thought, like a child wanting to be told that the bogey-man would not get him.

"I am sure it will, Sire. You have made it quite clear, I imagine, that Her Majesty must not be permitted to enter the Abbey?"

"I have given my orders," the King said, "but as you well know, she is determined to make me look a fool."

"You have never lacked courage, Sire," the Earl said.

"No, that is true," the King agreed.

Underneath his fat and over-indulged appearance the Earl knew that he was not only kind and good-natured, but also unusually sensitive.

Nearly twenty-five years ago he had refused to attend another boxing match after seeing a prize-fighter killed in the ring at Brighton.

He had an aversion to animals being tortured for sport, and because he was against bull-baiting and cock-fighting they had to a great extent gone out of fashion amongst the gentlemen of the *Beau Monde*.

Above all, a fact which no-one now seemed to remember, he had done everything in his power to assuage the harshness of the Criminal Code and had commuted an innumerable number of death sentences.

"Do you know what happened when I was staying at the Pavilion?" Sir Robert Peel the Home Secretary had asked the Earl the previous year.

"No—what did happen?" the Earl enquired.

"The King sent for me long after midnight."

"What on earth for?" the Earl asked.

"Apparently the imminent execution of a certain criminal had so upset His Majesty that he could not sleep.

"'You must pardon him, Sir Robert,' he said to me. 'You quite understand? You must pardon him.'"

"What did you do?"

Sir Robert smiled.

"Naturally I agreed to a pardon and the King kissed me excitedly!"

"Good God!" the Earl exclaimed.

"Then as he did so he noticed my dressing-gown."

"Your dressing-gown?"

"It was rather an old one," Sir Robert explained self-consciously, "but His Majesty exclaimed:

" 'Peel, where did you get that dressing-gown? I will show you what a dressing-gown ought to be.' "

"I imagine he produced one of his own," the Earl said with a smile.

"That is exactly what he did," Sir Robert answered, "and he made me put it on."

The King was an extraordinary mixture of brilliance, wit, and uncontrolled emotionalism.

Yet even his worst enemy could not have wished upon him a worse fate than to be married to the Princess Caroline of Brunswick.

The Earl, who had often met her, had found her a short, coarse, vulgar, unbalanced woman who could never at any time have attracted anyone so fastidious as the "First Gentleman of Europe."

Now he found himself hoping with a fervency that was unusual for him that she would in fact not spoil the Coronation.

"I have made two very stupid mistakes in my life, Meltham," the King reflected.

"Only two, Sire?" the Earl enquired, "most of us make a great many more."

"Two that mattered," the King answered. "One was to get married, the other to stage that damned Trial."

"I agree with you, Sire, but there is nothing you can do about it now."

"All I can say to you, Meltham," the King said impressively, "is for God's sake be careful whom you take for a wife."

"I have learnt by your example, Sire, and I have no intention of getting married."

"You are right! Absolutely right!" the King approved. "A man can have women in his life without marriage, but a wife can be the very devil!"

Driving away from Carlton House, the Earl was convinced, though he had not said so to the King, that the Queen would try to enter Westminster Abbey.

Lord Hood, who was Chamberlain to her, had

already said openly that he would get her in if he
had to drop her down from the Tower.

But those in charge of the King's arrangements
were equally determined that she should not spoil
the ceremony for which Parliament had voted the
incredible sum of £243,000.

On leaving Carlton House the Earl went to luncheon at his Club in St. James's.

As he entered he found a close friend, Captain
Charles Kepple, resplendent in the uniform of the
House-Hold Cavalry sitting in the Morning-Room with
a glass in his hand.

"I tried to see you yesterday, Vidal," he said, "but
heard you were out of London."

"I was in the country, Charles," the Earl replied,
"inspecting my new property."

He sat down in a chair opposite his friend and
signalled the waiter to bring him a glass of sherry.

"Your new property?" Charles Kepple exclaimed.
"Then it is true! I had heard you had won Wroxley's
Estate at cards."

"For once rumour is correct," the Earl answered.

"Good Heavens!" his friend exclaimed. "What
would you want with any more properties? You own
half the British Isles as it is!"

The Earl laughed.

"As usual, Charles, you exaggerate."

"It is not like you to gamble so high," Charles
Kepple said. "You have always declared it to be a
mug's game."

"So it is!" the Earl replied. "I can amuse myself
far more easily and more cheaply than by throwing
my money away on baize tables in the company of
nit-wits."

"There I agree with you," Charles Kepple said.
"Then why on this occasion?"

The Earl sipped his sherry before he replied:

"I was just entering the Card-Room to see who
was there when I met Darleigh coming out.

" 'Are you leaving?' I asked.

"'If there is one thing I cannot stand,' His Lordship replied, 'it is seeing that outsider, Crawthorne, plucking young chickens. It makes me sick!'"

"I am not surprised," Charles Kepple ejaculated. "It makes all of us sick. He gets them into his clutches, pretends he is their friend, and then rolls them for every penny they possess."

"That is just what he was doing last week," the Earl said. "I walked up to the table and saw he had two real greenhorns with him; boys who had never played anything more exciting than 'Snap' or 'Beggar my neighbour' before they came to London."

"In Crawthorne's hands they will learn the hard way," Charles Kepple remarked dryly.

"They were learning," the Earl said grimly, "and Wroxley was there too. He is older and I never did much care for the young man. At the same time I only had to look at him to realise that he was to let in the pockets and had not the guts to walk away."

"Crawthorne never lets them go," Charles Kepple said.

"When I reached the table," the Earl went on, "I heard Crawthorne say:

"'Come on, Giles. It is not like you to be chicken-hearted.' I knew by the look in his eyes and the way he was wetting his lips with the tip of his tongue he was onto a good thing."

"He is not really a clever gambler," Charles Kepple interposed. "As you noticed, Vidal, when he is excited he always gives himself away."

"I joined in the game, which rather surprised them," the Earl went on. "I had no idea what Wroxley was putting up as collateral. But when I won I saw the fury on Crawthorne's face."

"I wish I had been there!" Charles Kepple cried.

"I rose from the table," the Earl went on, "and suggested to the two greenhorns that they have a drink with me."

"Did they accept?" Charles Kepple asked.

"With alacrity. They had been mesmerised by

Crawthorne. I paid for their drinks and sent them home to their mothers!"

"Crawthorne must have wanted to murder you!"

"I had no idea what I had won until the Steward in the Card-Room informed me it was Wroxley Priory!"

Charles Kepple threw back his head and laughed.

"Is not that just like you, Vidal?" he said. "You win a large Estate and you did not even realise for what you were bidding!"

"I know now," the Earl said quietly.

"I seem to have heard of Wroxley Priory," Charles Kepple said, "although I cannot think how. Or is it that I just know the name?"

The Earl changed the subject.

"I have just come from the King. I am sorry for him, Charles, he is extremely worried and apprehensive as to what will happen tomorrow."

"You mean how will the Queen behave?" Charles Kepple asked.

"Exactly! He is haunted by the fear that she will spoil the 'splendid ceremony, lavish, dignified, and memorable,' on which he had set his heart."

"She will if she can!" Charles Kepple said prophetically.

"My heart bleeds for him," the Earl went on. "He is full of vanity, but no man deserves to suffer as he has suffered from that abominable woman!"

"Has it put you off marriage?" Charles Kepple asked with a grin.

"There is no reason for me to be put off more than I am already," the Earl replied. "As I told the King, I have no intention of marrying."

"You will have to one day," his friend said. "What about an heir?"

"I think you have forgotten that I have a younger brother," the Earl replied, "an extremely sensible and able man."

"That is true," Charles Kepple agreed. "If ever there was a good soldier it is Jonathan. I served with him.

He is as brave as a lion and his troopers would follow him anywhere."

"He will step very ably into my shoes," the Earl said.

"Good God, Vidal! You talk as if you were going to die tomorrow."

"On the contrary," the Earl said, "I intend to amuse myself and enjoy not one woman, but a considerable number before I weary of the joys of life."

He finished his glass of sherry and the waiter brought him another.

"I am still thinking of our Monarch," he said. "I know, Charles, he would appreciate it if you were to call in and see him during the afternoon. This is not a time when he should be alone. We all know how emotional he is."

Charles Kepple laughed.

"And unstable. He is so on edge that he seized Sir Benjamin Bloomfield—the innocuous Keeper of the Privy Purse—by the collar and gave him a good shake!"

"He is often unpredictable," the Earl remarked.

"Did you hear what the Duke of Wellington said about him?" Charles Kepple enquired.

"No, what did he say?"

"He said, 'The King is the most extraordinary compound of talent, wit, buffoonery, obstinacy, and good feeling, in short a medley of the most opposing qualities with a greater preponderance of good I have ever known.'"

The Earl laughed.

"I think that sums up our friend very well. I like him—I always have!"

"And he likes you," Charles Kepple said. "I think in a way he relies on you, Vidal, and at the same time he admires you."

The Earl did not answer and he went on:

"You are all the things he would like to be—dashing, wildly attractive to women, extremely intelligent, a sportsman, and at the same time cynical, ruthless,

and, like him, determined when it comes to something you want."

"You flatter me!" the Earl said dryly.

"I am just speaking the truth," Charles Kepple
smiled. "Let us go in to luncheon and, as you suggest, I will call at Carlton House. What are you doing
this afternoon?"

"I have plans," the Earl answered enigmatically, but
he did not elucidate further.

When luncheon was over he drove his phaeton with
an expertise that was remarkable through the traffic
in Piccadilly towards Chelsea.

Almost every pedestrian stopped to stare at the
Earl with his hat at an angle and controlling the
finest horse-flesh any man could desire.

He travelled past Apsley House where the Duke of
Wellington lived and down Sloane Street to some
quiet houses clustered round the Royal Hospital which
had been erected by Charles II for old soldiers.

Here in small elegant houses the Gentlemen of the
Beau Monde kept the lovely "Sylphides" who attracted
their attention.

Mademoiselle Désirée Lafette had been acclaimed
by the theatre-goers of London as a rising actress of
great talent.

She had many accomplishments and could entertain
both as a singer and a dancer.

At the moment she was playing the lead in one of
Sheridan's witty Conversation Pieces at His Majesty's
Theatre, and the Earl found her beguiling not only on
but off the stage.

As he expected, Désirée was resting at three o'clock
in the afternoon, preparing herself for the arduous
part she would play later in the evening.

He handed his hat and cloak to the rather theatri-
cal-looking maid-servant who had opened the door to
him, and without waiting to be announced walked
upstairs.

He found as he had expected *Mademoiselle* Lafette
reclining on a *chaise-longue* at the foot of the elab-

orately draped bed in her elegant if somewhat over-decorated bed-room.

She gave a cry of delight when he entered the room and rose from the couch to run towards him eagerly, her arms out-stretched, her dark hair which reached far below her waist flowing back from her attractive, piquant little face.

Désirée was not beautiful, but she had a French-woman's allure and a fascinating countenance which men found hard to forget.

"*Mon cher,* I was hopin' so much that you would come to see me *aujourd'hui,*" she said in her musical voice with a broken accent which the play-goers found irresistible.

She put her arms round the Earl's neck. He kissed her forehead and the tip of her nose before he said good-humouredly:

"Do not throttle me, Désirée! It is damned hot this afternoon."

"*Tiens,* then I must not wear so many clothes!" she answered.

The Earl saw she was wearing a négligée of pink gauze which made no attempt to conceal her naked-ness. Round her neck was the diamond necklace he had given to her the previous week.

"You look very alluring," he said. "And here is some-thing to add to your collection."

He drew a box from his pocket as he spoke and put it into her hands.

Then as he divested himself of his coat to throw it down onto a chair he watched with a twinkle in his eyes the excitement on Désirée's face.

The open box revealed a diamond bracelet which glittered in the sunshine coming through the window.

"*C'est superb! Merci! Merci, mon brave.* It is, as you know, what I have longed to possess."

She moved swiftly towards him with a grace which came from long years of learning ballet to put her arms round his neck.

"The jewels are very marvellous," she said, "but

what are jewels unless you are with me? I was *très
triste* yesterday because *je ne t'ai pas vu.*"

The Earl's arms went round her and he felt her
body moving sensuously against him.

He said with a smile:

"You are right, Désirée, you are over-dressed!"

With experienced hands he removed first the necklace and then the diaphanous gauze négligée.

It was nearly five o'clock before the Earl drove his
phaeton back from Chelsea to Meltham House in Park
Lane.

There was a cynical smile on his lips as he tooled
his horses through the traffic, and he was apparently
so absorbed in his thoughts that he did not see various
elegantly gloved hands waving to him as he passed
through the Park.

Meltham House was a magnificent edifice which
had been built by his grandfather half-way down Park
Lane.

It was surrounded by its own garden, the rooms
were vast and had the proportions and elegance which
the King had insisted upon at Carlton House.

The Adam Brothers had been responsible for the
building and for the exquisite decoration of the Hall,
the Salons, and the huge Banqueting-Room.

The Library was considered one of the best exam-
ples of their work, and the Earl's father had con-
tributed to the house its fine collection of Dutch pictures which were only surpassed by those which had
been acquired by the King when he was Prince of
Wales.

The Earl walked into the house to be greeted by
his Butler and six footmen all wearing the Meltham
livery of green and gold which was as well known in
London as that of the Royal servants.

"Lady Imogen is in the Silver Salon, My Lord,"
the Butler said in a respectful tone as he took His
Lordship's hat.

"Lady Imogen?" There was a frown between the Earl's eyes and his lips tightened.

"Her Ladyship has been waiting for over an hour, M'Lord."

The Earl seemed about to say something, then changed his mind.

Instead he walked across the marble Hall and an attentive flunkey opened the door to the Silver Salon.

It was a charming room over-looking the garden and there were flowers on the side-tables which gave it a feminine air and seemed to accentuate the beauty of the woman who rose from a chair at his entrance and held out her hands to him.

Lady Imogen Berrington was undoubtedly one of the most beautiful women in London.

The daughter of the Duke of Ruckton, she had been married almost out of the School-Room and widowed the previous year when her husband had been killed in an unnecessary and drunken duel in which he never should have taken part.

Before his death Lady Imogen had decided he was a bore, and they had little in common, and to all intents and purposes she had gone her own way.

For the past six months that way had led her to the Earl.

While at first he had found her extremely attractive and enjoyed the wild, passionate overtures she made to him, he was beginning to find that she was far too possessive.

In their relationship they had very different objectives.

The Earl was not only an extremely clever man, he was also very experienced where women were concerned.

Women had been in love with him ever since he was a boy, and when he inherited his vast Estates and the great wealth which made him one of the richest men in the country, he would have been very obtuse if he had not realised his own worth.

He knew he had only to raise his finger for any

marriageable woman in the Kingdom to fall into his arms.

Mamas with eligible daughters wooed him on their knees, and because he was so attractive as a man it would have been difficult to find a bed-room door that would not open at his touch.

He was well aware that Lady Imogen was not content with their present relationship. She wanted marriage and that was the one thing he did not intend to give her.

She was however stalking him with a persistence that he himself had never had to expend in pursuit of a woman.

He had the suspicion that she intended to inveigle him into marrying her simply by swaying public opinion in her favour.

While the *Beau Monde* were prepared to close their eyes to innumerable liaisons amongst themselves, they disliked open scandals.

The Earl guessed that Imogen was trying to manoeuvre him into a position where unless he behaved like a cad he would have to make reparation for the damage he had done her good name by proffering her a wedding ring.

Only Imogen, he thought as he entered the Silver Salon, would have the audacity to call unaccompanied at a bachelor's establishment!

Only Imogen would look at him in just that way with a fire smouldering in her eyes and her lips parted provocatively.

"I thought you had forgotten my existence," she said in a low, rather husky voice.

"I have been out of London," the Earl said, and wondered irritably to how many more people he would have to explain his absence.

"So I heard," Lady Imogen answered. "I missed you last night at the Fitzgeralds' Ball."

"Which I would not have attended had I been in London."

"They expected you."

"A great many people do that."

He stood looking at her as she stepped towards him.

"I always expect you," she said softly, "and lately you have been neglecting me."

The Earl moved away to put out his hand towards the bell-pull.

"You would like tea?" he suggested. "And I could do with a drink."

The door was opened almost instantly and he gave the order while Lady Imogen seated herself on one of the gold-framed chairs knowing that it was a fitting back-ground for her green gown and her wide-brimmed bonnet trimmed with feathers.

Her hair was a fiery red with touches of gold in it and her large dark-fringed eyes were green.

She had been painted by all the great artists and acclaimed to be the most beautiful subject they had known since Emma Hamilton had been immortalised by Romney.

"I want to talk to you, Vidal," Lady Imogen said.

Her voice was so full of intimate under-tones that the Earl exclaimed with an expression of relief:

"Ah! Here is the tea."

The Butler had evidently expected that tea would be required and it was brought into the room by three footmen.

The silver shone almost blindingly as the tray was set down beside Lady Imogen and an assortment of sandwiches, cakes, and biscuits was offered to her.

The Earl preferred a glass of claret. When the servants had withdrawn and Lady Imogen was pouring the tea he said:

"You should not come here alone, Imogen, as you well know."

"You used to ask me to do so when we first met," she replied.

This was true and the Earl could not deny it.

In the first fire of their relationship they had both

forgotten any notions of propriety and had laid aside all restraint.

Of all the women to whom the Earl had made love, Lady Imogen was perhaps the most passionate and the most insatiable.

She behaved at times almost like a tigress, and he reflected to himself now: 'The fire that burns too brightly is often the quickest to be extinguished.'

But he had the uncomfortable feeling that it would not be easy to rid himself of Imogen's fire.

"I want to talk to you," Lady Imogen said again, after she had sipped a cup of China tea, "because, Vidal, people are gossiping about us."

"Is that anything unusual?" the Earl asked. "You have set the town alight, Imogen, ever since you left the School-Room, and if people talk about me it is because they have nothing better to do!"

"They are talking about us—together," Lady Imogen said softly, "and I think, dearest Vidal, we should do—something about it."

There was no mistaking the invitation in the glance she gave him.

The Earl sighed.

He had hoped that Imogen would realise since he had been less attentive to her for the last few weeks that it was time to bring to a close what had undoubtedly been a very pleasant episode in both their lives.

But it had been only an episode as far as he was concerned, and he was quite determined that it should be nothing more.

At the same time, like all men, he disliked scenes, and he had no wish to actually put into words what to a more perceptive and sensitive woman would have been very obvious.

"Now listen, Imogen . . ." he began.

As he spoke the door opened.

"Miss Celesta Wroxley, My Lord!" the Butler announced and the Earl turned in amazement.

Standing in the doorway was Celesta looking very young and frightened.

The Earl rose to his feet and as she came slowly towards him he saw that her hands were trembling and she was unnaturally pale.

"This is a surprise, Miss Wroxley!" the Earl said politely. "May I welcome you to Meltham House?"

Celesta curtsied. Then as she rose with an obvious effort she said:

"Could I . . . see Your Lordship . . . alone? There is . . . something I must ask of . . . you."

"Of course," the Earl agreed. "But will you not first sit down and have some tea? Imogen, may I introduce Miss Celesta Wroxley—Lady Imogen Berrington!"

Lady Imogen inclined her head so slightly as to be insulting while Celesta dropped a nervous curtsy.

She sat down as if compelled to do so on the very edge of a chair.

A footman had already brought another cup and Lady Imogen poured out the tea.

"Do you take milk and sugar, Miss Wroxley?" she asked in a voice of someone offering arsenic.

"No, thank you," Celesta replied.

Her voice was hardly audible.

The footman handed to Celesta the tea which Lady Imogen had poured out. She held the cup and saucer in her hands as if uncertain what to do with them.

She was offered sandwiches and cake and declined them both.

"I did not expect to see you in London," the Earl said conversationally.

"N-no."

"I can see that Miss Wroxley comes from the country," Lady Imogen said meaningfully.

Her glance at Celesta took in scornfully the unfashionable gown which had been made by Nana, the plain bonnet trimmed only with blue ribbons.

"I expect you have heard," the Earl said to Lady Imogen, "that I have lately acquired Wroxley Priory.

It is a very fine and beautiful house which was once a Monastery. As it is less than two hours from London and on the road to Dover I thought it might be useful."

"But of course!" Lady Imogen exclaimed. "It is a perfect distance away! We could have parties from Saturday to Monday, or indeed, Vidal, we might give a Ball. Think how amusing that would be! And in a Priory what could be more appropriate than if everyone wore fancy dress?"

She gave an affected little laugh.

"I might come as the family ghost—I am sure there is one—all in flowing white with a cross of blood-red rubies, if you are prepared to give me one!"

She smiled in a seductive manner at the Earl. Then turning to Celesta she said:

"The Earl and I have such amusing ideas as to how we can entertain and amuse our guests. Conventional parties are so boring! Do you not find them so?"

"I do not go fo ... parties," Celesta replied.

"No?" Lady Imogen raised her eye-brows.

Then as if it was of the utmost indifference to her she turned again towards the Earl and said:

"I must see this new acquisition of yours, Vidal, at once. When will you take me to the Priory?"

"I have no immediate plans to go there again," the Earl said coldly. "If you have finished your tea, Miss Wroxley, perhaps you would come with me into the Library?"

Celesta rose quickly and put down her cup and saucer.

"I will wait for you," Lady Imogen said softly to the Earl.

"It is unnecessary," he replied. "I have some letters to write before I change for dinner. Good-bye, Imogen."

"I shall see you tomorrow night at your party," Lady Imogen said. "We are all looking forward to it and I am sure, Vidal, you will want me to help with the arrangements earlier in the day."

"That will not be necessary," he answered. "Everything has been already arranged and as you know, I shall be at the Coronation."

"Of course. How stupid of me! We will all be in the Abbey!" Lady Imogen exclaimed. "Smile at me, Vidal, or I shall find the ceremony a dead bore!"

The Earl did not answer. He turned away to follow Celesta across the room.

He opened the door and she passed through it. Then as he would have gone after her, he found Imogen's hands on his arm pulling him back into the Salon.

He paused because without using force it was impossible not to do so.

Then in a low voice but which was perfectly audible to Celesta outside in the Hall, Lady Imogen said:

"Who is the milk-maid, Vidal? Did you ever see such an antiquated gown made of cheese-cloth, and a bonnet that one of my house-maids might wear? Oh, darling, you are losing your touch, if that is what you find attractive in the country amongst the turnips!"

The Earl shook himself free of Lady Imogen's clinging hands.

He did not answer her but she knew by the expression on his face that he was angry.

Then he walked from the Salon, pulling the door sharply to behind him.

Celesta was waiting for him and he put his hand under her arm to draw her down the long passage to the Library where he habitually sat.

It was very different from the Library at the Priory, and yet to Celesta it had a warmer and more friendly atmosphere about it than the Salon.

She was still trembling as she entered the room and a flunkey shut the door behind them.

She thought to herself that she should feel humiliated by Lady Imogen's description of her appearance, but somehow it did not matter.

She was far too worried and distraught by what

she had come to ask the Earl to be perturbed by anything a stranger could say about her.

At the same time she could not help thinking that
the Earl's suggestion he had made to her the night
before was no more than some obscure jest on his part.

The beautiful, sophisticated lady who talked to him
so familiarly was obviously the type of woman he
admired.

Never in her wildest dreams, she thought humbly,
had she imagined that anyone could be so lovely, so
smart, or so elegant.

The thoughts rushed through her mind, and it was
a pale and very frightened little face that she turned
towards the Earl as he came across the room towards
her.

Her eyes seemed unnaturally large in her face and
there was an expression of pleading in them which
made the Earl ask:

"What has happened? Tell me what has upset you."

"I have come to . . . ask for your . . . help," Celesta
answered. "It is . . . wrong of me, I know, but there
is . . . no-where else I can go and . . . no-one else I can
. . . ask."

There was a throb in her voice which told the Earl
she was not far from tears.

"What has happened?" he asked again.

"Giles . . . my brother, is in . . . prison," Celesta
answered.

Chapter Four

Celesta had been awakened early in the morning by Nana coming into her room with a letter in her hands.

She pulled back the curtains, saying:

"Wake up, Miss Celesta! There's a man who's brought a letter from Sir Giles and he says as it's urgent!"

"Giles?" Celesta exclaimed, sitting up in bed.

She held out her hands for it and saw that it was rather dirty, as if it had been crumpled in a pocket.

"Would you believe it?" Nana asked. "The man has demanded a sovereign for delivering it to us!"

"There must be some mistake!" Celesta exclaimed.

"No! He says he 'as put himself to considerable inconvenience to bring it and Sir Giles promised we'd pay him a sovereign on delivery."

"Giles must be demented if he thinks we have that sort of money!" Celesta exclaimed. "Surely, Nana, you told the man that a sovereign would be an exorbitant amount to ask?"

Nana did not speak and Celesta said accusingly:

"You paid him, Nana?"

"Well, it was from Master Giles," Nana said almost shame-facedly, "and the man seemed to think 'twas very urgent. He must be in some sort of trouble and it worries me to think of it."

Celesta opened the letter and found that Nana was right. Giles was in trouble.

He had written in his untidy hand:

*I am in the Fleet Prison for debt. Come to me
immediately and bring all the money you can
lay your hands on, and hurry, Celesta, hurry
for God's sake!*

                                              Giles

Celesta read the letter through as if she could hardly believe her eyes and then as Nana watched apprehensively at the end of the bed, she handed the letter
to her.

"Oh, my baby! My poor baby!" Nana murmured
after she had read the letter. "We must go to him,
Miss Celesta. We must go to him at once!"

"Yes, of course, Nana," Celesta agreed, getting out
of bed. "At the same time, we have little money to
take him."

That was certainly true because when Celesta had
dressed and they had counted every penny they had,
it amounted to only a few shillings over three pounds.

Celesta knew that Nana had been dipping into her
small savings for some time.

She had begged her not to do so, but when luxuries such as spring-chicken or leg of lamb appeared on
the menu, she knew that Nana would have paid for
it and that the one pound a week of her money, which
was all they had to spend, could not include such
expensive items of food.

She also had the suspicion that Nana deceived her
about the price of the materials she paid for her
gowns.

"This cannot have cost only six pence a yard!" she
would exclaim.

And although Nana persisted that it was the truth,
Celesta was sure that while the cost to her was six
pence a yard, Nana had paid the extra out of her own
pocket.

However they had little time at the moment to consider anything but the urgency of getting to London.

The first Dover Stage-coach passed through the village at half after ten and they were waiting anxious-

ly at The Blue Boar, which was the stopping place, for only five minutes before it hove into sight.

It was very crowded and although they managed to squeeze themselves in, the journey to London was by no means a comfortable one.

When the coach reached The White Bear in Piccadilly, it went no further and Nana and Celesta consulted together as to the best way to reach the Fleet Prison, which was situated between Ludgate Hill and Fleet Lane.

Finally, feeling that whilst it was extravagant there was nothing else they could do, Celesta took a hackney carriage.

The driver showed his surprise on being given their destination.

"Ye don't look th' sort of ladies what ought t' be callin' at a prison!" he remarked.

"But that is where we wish to go," Celesta said firmly.

She had intended to dismiss the carriage on arrival, but when she saw that the prison was situated in a Market she changed her mind.

The noise of the porters, the smell of rotting vegetables, the paper lying about the streets, and the rough neighbourhood made her feel that it might be impossible to find another hackney carriage after they had visited Giles.

The entrance to the prison, although it had been rebuilt, dated back to William the Conqueror.

The high walls, the barred windows, and the general air of gloom made Celesta, already apprehensive, feel even more afraid of the conditions in which they would find Giles.

The surly Turnkey asked them their business and when they explained that they wished to see Sir Giles Wroxley he said:

" 'E'll be in th' Master's side."

He opened the door for Celesta and Nana and instantly they were aware of the stench, unlike any-

thing they had ever smelt before, coming from a long
stone passage with rooms on either side.

The gaol seemed to be crowded, and as Celesta and
Nana followed the Turnkey the place suddenly
echoed with the defiant shouts of prisoners who ran
to the bars of their cells.

When they saw how young and pretty Celesta was
they shouted obscenities and made lewd suggestions.

Some of the men were three parts naked and Celesta could not help noticing that lying on straw or in
dirty beds there were women, sometimes flashily
dressed and sometimes wearing no clothes at all.

There were also dozens of children, while a number
of other people moving about who appeared to be
visitors seemed unperturbed by the hideous noise.

After they had passed what Celesta realised were
the cells of the poor debtors who could not pay for
their lodgings, they came to the Master's side, which
had rooms occupied by only one or two prisoners in
each.

Finally the Turnkey opened the door of a room
which appeared smaller than the others but where
Giles was sitting alone.

He raised his head apathetically as the door opened,
and when he saw Celesta he rose somewhat unsteadily to his feet.

"You have taken long enough to get here!" he said
disagreeably in a thick voice.

Celesta stared at her brother in horror.

He was unshaven, his cravat was a soiled, crumpled
rag round his neck, his coat although smartly cut was
stained and dirty as were his trousers which had been
originally pale yellow.

The air in the room was stale and there was an
unmade bed in one corner.

On the floor there were nearly a dozen bottles now
empty which had once contained gin or brandy.

"Oh . . . Master Giles . . . it can't be true!" Nana
exclaimed and burst into tears.

"Why in God's name have you brought her?" Giles asked Celesta.

"I could hardly come alone," she answered, "and as for taking a long time, we only received your letter this morning."

"Damnit! The lying swine!" Giles swore. "He is a runner who does errands for the prisoners and he promised to deliver it last week!"

"Have you been here that long?" Celesta asked, looking round the small room in horror.

"Ten days," Giles replied, "and it is the nearest thing to Hell that any man could endure on earth!"

"I can see that!" Celesta answered.

"Have you brought any money?"

The question was rough and urgent.

"Only a little, I am afraid."

Celesta opened her purse as she spoke.

To her astonishment Giles snatched it from her and stumbling across the room rattled on the door to attract the attention of the Turnkey.

"Let me out!" he ordered. "I want to go to the Whistling Shop."

"Oi thought that's where you'd want to go, me fine gentleman, as soon as ye could afford it!"

The Turnkey unlocked the door and Giles hurriedly disappeared.

Nana had a handkerchief to her eyes.

"How can this have happened?" she said. "Your poor father would turn in his grave if he knew of it!"

"Well, at any rate let us try to tidy up the place," Celesta suggested.

She was as horrified as Nana, but she felt no good could come of behaving emotionally, which she knew was one thing Giles disliked most.

Nana wiped her eyes and went towards the bed.

As was usual in a debtors' prison, furniture and bed-linen were all supplied by the prisoners.

Giles's sheets were creased and dirty and Nana looked round as if expecting to find another pair in the sparsity of the dark cell.

Celesta began to collect the bottles from the floor and stand them in a corner.

Giles had obviously been drinking before they arrived but all the bottles were now empty and she had the idea that the "Whistling Shop" meant somewhere where he could buy spirits.

Later she was to learn that spirits were not allowed in prison under any circumstances except by a Doctor's orders, but needless to say the regulation was a dead letter.

It was not sold openly, but there were rooms known to all the prisoners where it could be procured.

It was never asked for by name and if it had been, an applicant would not have received it. But if he whistled, it was immediately forthcoming.

There was a Coffee-Shop where those who could afford it could eat surprisingly good food, but the majority had to subsist on a starvation diet which was doled out to them by the Turnkeys who bullied those who could not pay.

There was also a system of parole for those who could pay a commission of five percent upon the amount of their charge.

This meant that a prisoner could move about freely within the confines of the Fleet, which included the Belle Savage Public-House selling fine ale.

The whole manner in which the Fleet Prison was administered was already being talked about as a disgrace to London. A report had been published in 1819 after there had been an enquiry in the House of Commons.

The prison contained within its walls 109 rooms, 89 of which were cells shared between two debtors each and 3 called Slips which were small and low and therefore accommodated only one prisoner. Giles was in one of these.

The rent for each room was one-third pence a week, payment of which was demanded quarterly, and if it was not paid the occupiers were turned out and put in the Common side, where there might be seven or eight prisoners to one cell.

Celesta of course did not know it, but there were at that time 209 people confined within the walls of the prison and yet there was no regular Physician or Surgeon in charge.

Despite the fact that one room was set aside as an Infirmary, no medicines were provided except those that could be paid for.

The three Turnkeys, who were rough, uncouth, often dishonest men, slept in the prison and yet every night there were scenes of rioting, drunkenness, and disorder.

The main reason for this was that there was no separation of women from men for they lived in the same cells.

What was more, women of what was called "bad character" were allowed into the prisons during the day and frequently stayed the night with the prisoners.

Husbands and wives slept together with other people in the cell, and one woman had a miscarriage in a crowded cell.

The behaviour of prisoners was something which had already been listened to with disgust by the House of Commons Committee.

Celesta mercifully was unaware of such horrors, but Nana had sized up the type of women she saw as they proceeded down the corridor, and the filth and dirt of the rooms, the cleaning of which was left to the prisoners.

"Master Giles can't stay in a place such as this," she said to Celesta.

She picked up a bucket of slops from a corner of the cell and pulling open the door asked the Turnkey where she could empty it.

"Cleaning up, are ye?" he asked. "'Tis a waste o' time! Th' drunks make more mess than any of 'em!"

Celesta heard what he said and felt for a moment as if she must faint.

How could Giles, her brother, have sunk so low that he was described by a Turnkey in a prison as a drunkard?

This was what his gay, irresponsible life in London had led him to. She knew that Nana was right when she said that it would break Sir Norman's heart to have seen him.

It was nearly half an hour before Giles came back.

He smelt of brandy and it was obvious that he had already been drinking. He set two bottles down on the table with exaggerated care in case they should upset.

"Now I want to talk to you, Celesta," he said.

She knew that the brandy had for the moment cleared his brain and his voice sounded less slurred than when they had first arrived.

"You know that I want to help you, Giles," Celesta answered. "But please do not drink so much of those horrible spirits. They will only make you feel worse!"

"What else is there for me to do in this ghastly place?" Giles asked.

"The most important thing," Celesta answered, "is to think of how we can get you out of it. Tell me . . . how much do you owe?"

There was a moment's pause and then Giles said in a voice that was defiant:

"Just under two-thousand pounds!"

"Giles!"

Celesta put up her hands.

"How can you have spent so much?"

"That is the sum which brought me here," he said. "The blasted tradesmen got together and dunned me! A Curse on all tradesmen!"

"And you lost the Priory . . . at cards," Celesta said in a small voice.

"Yes, damnit," he replied, "thanks to the Earl of Meltham! God blast his eyes!"

"You're not to swear like that in front of your sister, Master Giles," Nana said sharply. "It's not seemly, as you well know!"

"You stay out of this," Giles retorted.

But it seemed to Celesta that he looked a trifle ashamed as he spoke.

"How could you . . . gamble away the whole Estate?" she questioned.

"I was playing cards with Lord Crawthorne," Giles replied, "and Meltham butted in when he was not wanted. If Crawthorne had won, as he should have done, I could have bought the place back from him quite cheaply."

"But where would the money have come from?" Celesta asked.

There was silence and then Giles said:

"You have to help me, Celesta. You have to! There is no-one else!"

"You know I will do everything in my power," Celesta replied, "but where can I go? Who can I ask for money?"

"You will have to see Crawthorne," Giles said. "I have written to him several times, but I do not believe he has received my letters."

"I received the one you wrote to me."

"I cannot credit that Crawthorne, after all his protestations of friendship, would leave me here to rot!"

There was an uncertainty in Giles's voice which Celesta did not miss.

He poured himself some brandy from the bottle on the table into a dirty glass and swilled it down his throat. Then he said:

"Now listen to me, Celesta, you must go to Crawthorne. Tell him the condition I am in. Beg him to help me."

"But you say he has not answered your letters?"

"He will listen to you."

It seemed to Celesta as if Giles looked at her for the first time.

She was like a ray of sunshine against the dingy, dirty walls of the prison.

Her fair hair seemed to radiate light and her eyes were very blue beside the whiteness of her skin.

"He will listen to you," Giles said again positively. "Crawthorne likes pretty young women."

There was something in the way he spoke which made Celesta say hesitatingly:

"Is . . . is there . . . no-one else I could . . . approach . . . first? S-supposing I went to the . . . bank? Could I not obtain a loan?"

"And what would you offer as security?" Giles asked. "The Priory which we do not possess?"

"What about the money that . . . Papa left you?" Celesta asked. "When he died the capital was bringing in quite a considerable income every year. It was what we lived on!"

"It is gone! All gone!" Giles replied.

"At gaming?" Celesta asked him in horror.

"Crawthorne pocketed most of it. He taught me how to gamble, but such experience costs money!"

"If he took that money from you," Celesta said, "how can you expect that he will lend you anything now?"

"Because it is only fair he should give me back some of what he has had," Giles said defiantly. "You talk to him, Celesta. Plead with him and be nice to him!"

"Nice?" Celesta questioned.

"Oh, hell!" Giles said, pouring himself out another glass of brandy, "you know what I mean. A woman can do anything with a man if he fancies her!"

"You've no right to ask such things of your sister!" Nana said sharply.

She had been sitting on the edge of the bed listening to the conversation taking place between Giles and Celesta at the table.

Now she rose and came towards them.

"I'm taking Miss Celesta home," she said firmly. "I don't believe there's anything she can do, although it breaks my heart to say so, but London's no place for her!"

"You shut your mouth," Giles said roughly. "Celesta, do as I have told you. Go and see Crawthorne at his house in Charles Street. It is number six. Tell him where I am. Go down on your knees to him, but for God's sake get me out of here!"

There was an agonised note in Giles's voice now and for the first time he no longer looked rough and debauched, but young and rather frightened.

"I will do my best," Celesta promised, "my very best, Giles. I only hope that Lord Crawthorne will listen to me."

"He will listen to you," Giles said confidently.

Celesta drew in a deep breath.

"Please, Giles, tidy yourself and do not drink any more," she pleaded. "You used to be so smart and I admired you so much. I do not like to see you like this."

"I will look smart enough when I get out of here!" he answered, "and that is up to you, Celesta."

"Yes, I know," she murmured almost beneath her breath.

He made no effort to say good-bye or to touch her, for which she was grateful.

She could not bear to kiss him when he was smelling so strongly of spirits and there was a dark stubble on his chin and upper lip.

The Turnkey escorted them back the way they had come, past the cells where the inmates again shouted and yelled at them, using words which fortunately Celesta did not understand.

At last they passed through the outer door and found their hackney carriage waiting for them.

Only when they were inside and being driven away did Nana once again burst into tears.

"He was such a dear little boy," she kept saying.

But Celesta knew it was not only Giles's appearance that had upset her but the rough, uncouth way in which he had spoken, the manner in which he had sworn, and the fact that the Turnkey had referred to him as a drunkard.

There was little she could say to comfort the old woman who had adored Giles ever since his birth.

She herself was deeply shocked at Giles's depravity and the fact that he had appeared to have lost all pride in himself.

She had the feeling that Lord Crawthorne was to blame for everything.

She could remember how enthusiastic Giles had been about him; how he had talked of his kindness, his patronage, and his guidance when he had introduced him to London.

Now that she was older, Celesta knew that the women Giles had brought to the Priory to amuse Lord Crawthorne were not the type of females that her father would have tolerated in his house.

It was wrong for her brother to have asked them into his home when she was under the same roof.

Deep in her thoughts she found little to say to Nana as they drove through the crowded streets back towards Mayfair.

When the hackney carriage came to a standstill outside No. 6 Charles Street, it brought her back to the present with a start.

They were there and she had not yet planned what she would say to Lord Crawthorne, or how she should approach him.

She glanced at Nana and saw that the old woman was more composed.

"Stay with me, Nana," she said, "and on no account leave me alone with Lord Crawthorne."

"I'll do that, don't you worry, dearie," Nana said stoutly.

They stepped out onto the pavement. Celesta paid the driver and thanked him for having been so kind as to wait for them outside the prison.

"Oi hopes next time Oi drives you, Miss, Oi'll be ataking you to a better address!" the driver said with a smile.

He pocketed the tip that Celesta gave him on top of his fare and she realised with concern that there was only just enough money left in the bottom of her bag to get them back to Wroxley on the Stage-coach.

It was fortunate that everything she possessed had not been in her purse but only the sovereigns that she and Nana had collected for Giles.

"We shall have to walk to The White Bear after I have seen Lord Crawthorne," she told herself in a practical manner as they rang the bell.

The door was opened by a smart-looking servant with a disdainful air.

"Will you ask Lord Crawthorne if he will see Miss Celesta Wroxley?" Celesta asked.

The flunkey let them into the house, but obviously did not think them important enough to be shown into a Sitting-Room.

Instead he kept them standing in the Hall while he ascended to the first floor.

"His Lordship will see you, Miss," he said a few seconds later in a tone which suggested surprise.

Followed by Nana, Celesta climbed the stairs and the flunkey opened the door into a large, comfortable Salon.

Lord Crawthorne was seated in an arm-chair at the other end of it and for a moment he did not rise, but stayed where he was looking at Celesta.

For the first time she was looking at the man whom she had begun to believe in her heart was Giles's "evil genius" and somehow he was exactly as she had thought he would be.

Never had she seen a more debauched face.

Lord Crawthorne was over forty and the years of loose living had taken their toll.

There were dark bags beneath his eyes and deep-ly etched lines on his face gave him a sardonic ex-pression.

At the same time he was elegantly attired with a high cravat and a tightly fitting coat with a velvet collar. When he eventually rose, he was taller than Celesta had expected.

Slowly she walked towards him and she had the

feeling that he was inspecting her from head to toe, missing neither the beauty of her face nor the country-fied appearance of her clothes.

As she reached him he asked:

"Can you be Giles's sister? I had no idea that he had one!"

"I am indeed Giles's sister, My Lord," Celesta answered, "and I have come to speak to you about him."

"Sit down, my dear," Lord Crawthorne said genially, indicating a chair next to his own.

As Celesta obeyed him he glanced towards the end of the room where Nana had seated herself just inside the door on a hard chair.

"I think we can talk—alone," he said with a smile which Celesta found frightening.

"You are well aware, My Lord," she replied, "that I should be chaperoned. My Nurse and I have come here from the Fleet Prison."

"You have seen Giles!" Lord Crawthorne exclaimed.

"He tells me that he has written to you not once but several times. He is deeply perturbed that you have not answered his letters."

Lord Crawthorne spread out his hands in a gesture of helplessness. On one of them there glittered a signet ring set with a huge ruby.

"Giles's predicament is most distressing, but what can I do? I assure you, Miss Wroxley, that I am not a rich man."

"And yet you have won quite a lot of money from my brother," Celesta said.

"Money which we both spent most enjoyably on one entertainment or another," Lord Crawthorne replied, "and, as I dare say Giles has told you, he still owes me quite a considerable sum of money."

"How much?"

"Five hundred pounds!"

Celesta drew in her breath. Then she said:

"Giles is not likely to be able to pay you, My Lord, if he remains in a debtors' prison."

"And if he were free, do you think he would find the money to reimburse me? I doubt it!"

"But you were his friend!" Celesta cried. "You cannot leave him there! Please . . . please, My Lord, think of some way in which we can obtain his release!"

She bent forward as she spoke, her eyes on Lord Crawthorne's face, her fingers clenched together as she pleaded with him.

He looked at her and his eyes narrowed.

"You are very lovely!" he said softly, "so lovely that it surprises me Giles should have kept you hidden for so long."

"I live in the country, My Lord," Celesta said nervously.

"That is a situation that can easily be remedied. I think, Miss Wroxley, you should come to London."

"I have no wish to do that," Celesta replied.

"But I have every wish for you to do so," Lord Crawthorne smiled. "Celesta—I hope, as Giles is such a great friend of mine, that I may call you by your Christian name—I have a feeling we should get to know each other, and what could be more of a bond between us than our love for your brother?"

"If you love my brother, as you say, My Lord," Celesta answered, "you would free him from gaol. He cannot stay there! It is a horrible, filthy place and there is nothing he can do but drink!"

"You are very eloquent," Lord Crawthorne said, "and I think that I must listen to what you have to say about Giles. However this is neither the time nor the place for it."

As he spoke he glanced again towards Nana sitting very upright and obviously listening to everything that was said.

Lord Crawthorne looked at Celesta and there was an expression in his eyes which made her afraid.

"I will tell you what we can do," he said in a caressing voice. "We will dine together tonight and discuss your brother's dilemma."

"I have to . . . return to Wroxley," Celesta said
quickly. "Nana and I have . . . no-where to . . . stay
in London."

"If you go to The Griffon Hotel just round the corner in Queen Street," Lord Crawthorne answered, "I
will arrange for two comfortable rooms to be put at
your disposal. You will be my guest, and at seven
o'clock I will send a carriage for you. It will bring you
back here for dinner and I will listen to all you have
to say to me—alone!"

He accentuated the last word and as he did so he
smiled. Celesta felt an impulse to recoil from him as
if he were a reptile.

There was no mistaking the innuendo in his voice.

Innocent and unsophisticated though she was, she
was nevertheless aware that he was trying to trap
her.

He was looking at her in a manner which made her
feel as if he were already reaching out his arms towards her, and when his eyes rested on her lips she
felt so repelled that she wanted to run from the room
in sheer terror.

"I . . . I do not . . . think . . . I can . . . d-do . . .
t-that," she managed to stammer and her voice trembled as she spoke.

"It will all be arranged," Lord Crawthorne said.
"You are not to trouble your pretty head about it.
My man will call you a hackney carriage which will
carry you to the Hotel. He will then make arrangements in my name. I shall expect you later."

He paused to add:

"Need I say, little Celesta, that it will be with much
eagerness?"

He took her hand in his to raise it, as she thought,
to his lips.

She was wearing gloves, but instead he kissed the
inside of her wrist, his lips lingering greedily on the
softness of her skin.

She felt a shiver of horror run through her.

She could not explain to herself the repugnance he

aroused in her, but it was there, and when she tried
to take her hand away he would not let her go.

Still with his lips against her wrist he raised his
eyes to look up at her and she saw in them a lust
which shocked her into knowing that she was in the
very presence of evil.

"Until tonight!" Lord Crawthorne said silkily.

Somehow Celesta found her feet carrying her down
the stairs and out through the front door.

The servant found them a hackney carriage and
told it to drive to The Griffon Hotel.

No sooner had the horses started up than Celesta
put her head out the window on the other side and
cried:

"Go to Meltham House in Park Lane . . . and quickly!"

The man obeyed and it took them only a few mo-
ments to drive there.

As they went Celesta felt she was escaping from
something so frightening and so disgusting she could
hardly bear to think of it even to herself.

Her whole being was crying out with horror at the
idea that Giles had sent her deliberately to Lord
Crawthorne knowing what he was like; knowing what
his reaction would be.

And yet, she asked herself, what alternative was
there?

She was so bemused by what had occurred that
she did not feel over-awed by the magnificence of
Meltham House.

She could think of nothing but Lord Crawthorne
with the lustful expression on his face asking her to
dine with him, and she could still feel his lips against
her wrist.

In contrast to Lord Crawthorne, the Earl of Meltham seemed someone solid and secure, a man to whom
she could turn in her desperation.

"Your brother is in prison?" the Earl said with a
note of surprise in his voice. "Which prison?"

"The Fleet," Celesta answered.

"For debt, I suppose?" the Earl said. "How have you learnt this? You were not aware of it last night!"

"He bribed someone to bring us a letter this morning," Celesta explained. "He asked to see me and Nana and I at once came to London."

"You have been to the prison?" the question was sharp.

"Yes . . . we have just come from there."

The Earl did not speak and Celesta said in a low voice:

"It is terrible—ghastly! And Giles has deteriorated because he is so desperate. He has asked me to find the money for his release."

She could not look at the Earl as she spoke.

"And so he sent you to me!" he said, with what she thought was a dry note in his voice.

"No, no," Celesta answered quickly. "He asked me to visit Lord Crawthone, which I have . . . done."

"You have seen Crawthorne?"

"Yes . . . I have just come from his . . . house."

"You asked him to help your brother? After all it is mainly his fault that he is in a debtors' prison."

"I know that."

"And what did Lord Crawthorne say?"

"He . . . he asked me . . . to dine with him tonight . . . alone."

There was no mistaking the fear in Celesta's voice.

Now the Earl understood why she had been trembling when she entered the Salon and why her eyes were raised to him pleadingly, like a child who asked for help.

"This should never have happened!" he exclaimed and his voice was angry. "Why did you not come to me at once?"

"I . . . I did what . . . Giles told me to do. After all . . . Lord Crawthorne was supposed to be his friend."

"A friend who has not only won all his money from him, but intends to leave him where he is."

"I am . . . sure that is what . . . he will . . . do," Celesta agreed, "unless . . ."

"You will have nothing to do with Lord Crawthorne, Celesta, do you understand? You are not to see him or speak to him again!"

"I have no . . . wish to do so," she answered. "He is . . . horrible! Horrible!"

"He did not touch you?"

The question was sharp.

"No, Nana was with me. I made her stay in the room all the time I was with His Lordship. He told me we were to stay at a Hotel for which he would . . . pay, and that tonight I must . . . dine with him alone!"

"Now you understand why you should be chaperoned!"

The Earl paused and added:

"Or allow me to look after you."

Celesta turned her head aside.

The thought shot through her mind that she would far rather be under the protection of the Earl than at the mercy of Lord Crawthorne.

After a moment the Earl said quietly:

"I think you have been through enough for one day without being expected to make decisions of any sort. I am going to send you back to Wroxley."

He saw a light come into her eyes. Then she said hesitatingly:

"And . . . Giles?"

"I will see about Giles," the Earl said. "Stay here while I speak to my Secretary."

He walked from the room. Celesta put her hands to her breast as if to control the relief which swept over her and left her curiously weak.

Giles would be released and she would not have to dine with Lord Crawthorne!

She could hardly believe that the fear that had felt like a physical pain inside her was no longer there.

She undid the ribbons of her bonnet and took it off to lift her hair from her forehead. Then she rested her head against the back of the chair and closed her eyes.

She had not known it was possible to be so frightened of a man as she had been of Lord Crawthorne.

Yesterday she had believed she was afraid of the Earl, but now he seemed like a rock of strength to protect her against the horror of the evil she had seen in Lord Crawthorne's eyes.

'Thank you, God,' she whispered in her heart.

It was like coming out of a fog into the sunshine to know that she need battle no further on Giles's behalf.

The Earl came back into the Library and crossed the room to sit down in a chair beside Celesta.

"My Secretary is leaving immediately for the Fleet Prison," he said. "I have instructed him to pay your brother's debt and give him enough money for his immediate expenses."

Celesta drew in her breath and her eyes were shining as she looked up at the Earl.

"I have arranged for one of my carriages to convey your brother to you at the Cottage," he went on, "and another vehicle will take you and your Nurse there as soon as we have finished talking."

"What can I . . . say? How can I . . . thank you?" Celesta asked in a low voice.

"You already know I do nothing without expecting something in return," the Earl said in his mocking voice, "and so there is a condition that goes with my generosity."

"A . . . condition?" Celesta asked.

"It is quite a simple one," he said reassuringly. "It is that you and your brother will be my guests tomorrow night at the Ball I am giving after the Coronation."

Celesta stiffened.

"A . . . Ball?" she said. "But you know how . . . out of place I would be . . ."

"You will be nothing of the sort," the Earl contradicted. "You will be the most beautiful woman present and I intend my other guests to realise it."

There was a note in his voice which Celesta did not understand and she made a pathetic little gesture with her hands.

"How can you . . . imagine such a . . . thing when I shall be in the company of ladies who look like . . . Lady Imogen?" she asked almost piteously.

"You under-value yourself," the Earl answered. "I want you at my Ball, Celesta, and I think that the least you and your brother can do is to accede to my request."

He saw the troubled expression in her eyes and went on:

"If you are thinking about clothes, as all women do, you shall have the most beautiful gown in the whole of London!"

Celesta drew herself up proudly.

"I will not allow you to pay for my clothes, My Lord."

The Earl smiled.

"Is not that rather splitting hairs?"

"What you have paid for Giles is somehow different," she murmured.

Then as she knew the Earl was going to argue with her she said:

"I do have a gown. One in which you will not be . . . ashamed of me. It came from . . . Paris!"

"From your mother?"

Celesta nodded her head.

"And you were determined never to wear it?" the Earl said with a perception she had not expected of him, "yet at the moment you find it easier to take a gift from your mother rather than from me. Is that right?"

"It sounds as if I am very . . . ungrateful," Celesta said. "I do not know how to thank you . . . how to find words to tell you what I feel about your . . . kindness to Giles. It is just that I am . . . trying not to be too . . . involved with you."

The Earl smiled.

"I think we are both already very involved with
each other, Celesta, and there is nothing either of us
can do about it except attribute it to Fate."

He paused and as she did not speak he said:

"I am sure there is some literature about Fate and
its power over us poor humans that you will be able
to find either in the Library at Wroxley, or perhaps
here, let us accept it for what it is."

He was speaking in a beguiling manner which she
found somehow irresistible. Then he rose to his feet.

"Go home, Celesta," he said in a kind voice. "Go
to bed and forget your troubles. I want you to look
very beautiful tomorrow night, and do not be afraid
that anyone you meet in my house will ostracise you
because of your mother or for any other reason."

"You are . . . sure you are doing the . . . right thing
in inviting . . . me?" Celesta asked.

"I am doing what I want to do," the Earl replied,
"and that is always right where I am concerned."

Celesta picked up her bonnet from where she had
put it on an adjacent chair.

"I will try to . . . please you," she said in a low
voice. "And all the way home I shall be . . . thanking
you in my heart."

She drew in her breath and said a little helplessly:

"Perhaps . . . one day I shall be able to . . . repay
you."

The Earl was looking at her face. Now he said
very softly:

"You could do that now!"

She looked up at him in surprise.

"I want," the Earl said, "more than I have wanted
anything for a very long time in my life, to know if
your lips are really so soft and sweet as they seemed
to me yesterday in the peach-house."

Celesta's eyes met his.

Then almost as if she could not help herself, as if
she was compelled to do as he wished, she moved
towards him with the unself-conscious trust of a child.

"You have ... been so ... kind," she whispered.

His arm went round her and very gently his lips found hers.

It was very unlike the demanding, raffish manner in which he had kissed her on the previous day.

There was something tender and yet at the same time possessive in the manner in which his mouth held her captive.

She was not afraid and she was glad to give him what he desired because she was over-whelmed with gratitude.

Then it seemed to her as if something strange and inescapable happened within herself.

It was not just that he kissed her lips. It was as if he took possession of something deeper; as if her whole being responded to him and for a moment she had no identity of her own.

There was only the warm insistence of his mouth, tender and yet firm, as his lips seemed to take away thought.

Something strange and unaccountable seemed to flicker into life within her; incredibly, she wanted him to go on kissing her.

The Earl raised his head and she was free.

Then with a strange note in his voice she did not understand he said almost abruptly:

"You must go, Celesta. Is your Nurse waiting for you?"

"She ... she is ... in the hall," Celesta answered, feeling as if she could not understand his question or force herself to speak naturally.

"The carriage will be at the door," the Earl said.

Then they were walking down the corridor towards Nana and Celesta wondered why she felt as if her heart had turned several somersaults and was no longer in its right place.

Chapter Five

The King arrived half an hour late at Westminster Hall for his Coronation.

It was not his fault: Lord Gwydyr, the Acting Great Lord Chamberlain, had torn his clothes while dressing and therefore was forced to keep His Majesty waiting.

The bells of St. Margaret's, which pealed every half an hour from midnight until dawn, were drowned by the boom of the cannons firing across the river and the rockets exploding into the sky.

When the King appeared in his robes wearing a brown wig, the thick curls of which fell over his forehead and the nape of his neck, he looked as the Earl had expected, extremely impressive.

He had a dignity which silenced his critics.

The young people in particular who had gone expecting to laugh were taken by surprise and found themselves affected in a manner which they had not anticipated.

Indeed the whole scene impressed the spectators with its dignity and splendour.

The King's friends, like the Earl, could not help feeling triumphant that once again His Majesty's excellent taste had confounded his enemies, who had never ceased to grumble and snigger about the Coronation.

The Procession to the Abbey was led by the King's Herb-Woman and six young attendants who in accordance with the centuries-old tradition strewed the way with herbs and heavily scented flowers as a precaution against the plague.

The Barons of the Cinque Ports carried a canopy of gold, but the King had instructed them not to hold it over his head so that he could be seen by the people on the roof-tops.

His Majesty was preceded by three Bishops and in front of the Bishops were the Officers of State with the crown, orb, sceptre, and sword of State.

"Messrs. Rundell, Bridge, and Company," one of the Royal House-Hold whispered to the Earl, "are wondering if they will ever get paid for the Regalia!"

The Earl could not help smiling.

"How much are they owed?" he asked.

"Thirty-three thousand pounds!" was the reply, and the Earl's smile was very cynical as he remarked:

"I think their fears are well founded!"

The Earl and his fellow-Peers marched in Procession in order of seniority and they were followed by the Dignitaries of the City of London, who were almost as impressive with their chains and emblems of Office.

Twice the King stopped to give his two pages time to unfold and display his crimson-velvet, gold-embroidered train.

"Hold it wider," the Earl heard him say to them in a clear voice.

The Procession reached the West door of the Abbey at eleven o'clock.

As the King stepped inside the building the choir burst into the "Hallelujah Chorus" and the Congregation rose and cheered.

The Ceremony lasted for almost five hours and it was exceedingly hot.

The King looked very pale and more than once the Earl thought he seemed likely to collapse. But he was revived by sal volatile and a large number of those taking part would have welcomed something stronger!

The King did not falter during the Crowning Ceremony and when this had taken place, the Peers waved

their coronets and with everyone present waving caps
and handkerchiefs shouted at the top of their voices:

"God Bless the King!"

As the Premier Earl present, the Earl of Denbeigh
performed homage to the King, first repeating the
Oath of Allegiance, kissing his hand and left cheek
and touching with his fingers the crown on his head.

While this was taking place the Earl heard a voice
whisper in his ear:

"The Queen is trying to enter the Abbey!"

"Damnit!" the Earl replied, "I hope they are keeping her out!"

"I think it will be all right," his informant replied.

The Earl found himself worrying that Her Majesty
would effect an entrance and upset the King, who,
despite the heat and the weight of his robes, was
obviously enjoying not only the Ceremony but the
sincerity of the acclamations.

He had in fact been astounded that on the way to
the Abbey he had been applauded by the populace.

He was so used to hearing himself booed, hissed,
or shouted at by the London mob that it was like a
glass of champagne for him to feel that for once his
subjects were pleased with him.

The Queen on the other hand had lost the fickle
sympathy of those who had supported her all through
the Trial.

She set out for the Abbey as planned in her Coach
of State drawn by six bay horses.

Lady Hood and Lady Anne Hamilton sat opposite
her, while Lord Hood followed in another carriage.

But her reception for the first time was far from
enthusiastic.

Most of the spectators in the stands watched her in
silence, and the scattered shouts of "The Queen for
ever!" were drowned by loud whistling.

Discouraged by the attitude of the crowd, the Queen
stopped her carriage and looked about her.

When it moved forward again it drew up close to

the West door of Westminster Abbey, which was hurriedly closed amidst much confusion.

The Queen stepped out of the carriage and, leaning on Lord Hood's arm, approached two other doors which also shut in her face and were guarded by hefty prize-fighters.

"Am I to understand that you refuse Her Majesty admission?" Lord Hood asked.

"We only act in accordance with orders," the Door-Keeper replied.

The Queen laughed loudly.

Finally she was turned away by one of the Gold Staffs and as she drove away with the roof of her landau open there were a few shouts and hisses from the crowd.

Some people called out, "Go away!" "Go back to Como!" or "Back to Bergami," but otherwise she caused no more stir, and the danger of her upsetting the King was over.

"She has gone!" someone reported to the Earl in the Abbey.

"Thank God for that!" the Earl replied.

"Amen! And a plague on all women!" his informant murmured.

He obviously expected the Earl to agree with him and when there was no response, he moved back to his seat.

Soon after four o'clock the King, followed by his Peers, proceeded back to Westminster Hall for the Coronation Banquet.

"You must admit," the Earl said to the Noblemen beside him, "that when the English put on a spectacle, they do it well."

He looked as he spoke at the other Peers, wearing, like himself, their ermine-trimmed robes and coronets, at the Privy Councillors, the Knights of the Bath, and the Officers of State, all in the most spectacular dress.

The double row of Galleries on each side of the Hall were filled with all the most distinguished and beautiful Peeresses vying with each other in the mag-

nificence of their apparel and the splendour of their
gowns.

Some of them appeared to be literally ablaze with
diamonds.

"It is certainly impressive!" the Peer to whom the
Earl had spoken agreed. "I am told that Prince Es-
terhazy, the Austrian Ambassador, is wearing jewels
estimated at eight thousand pounds!"

Once the King had settled himself down at the
table, under a red and gold canopy, the meal was
brought in by a procession of House-Hold Officials,
while the Duke of Wellington, the Lord High Con-
stable, the Marquis of Anglesey, the Lord High Steward, and Lord Howard of Effingham, the Deputy
Earl Marshal appeared on horseback.

The Deputy Earl Marshal had trouble with his
horse and swore at it in a voice that resounded round
the Hall.

The King's Champion in full armour had, however,
taken the precaution of borrowing a white charger
from Asheley's Circus, who, being used to confined
spaces and cheering crowds, behaved perfectly.

The Earl with the Peers and the Bishops at the long
table in the centre of the Hall rose to drink His
Majesty's health and the King stood up to thank them
for their good wishes.

The Earl of Denbeigh served turtle soup to the
King and to the Royal Dukes and the Earl of Chiches-
ter cut up a pineapple weighing eleven pounds.

It was half past seven before the King retired from
the Hall to return to Carlton House.

It was then that the Peers and the Bishops were at
last allowed to sit down and enjoy the Banquet.

"I do not mind telling you," the Earl said to a friend
sitting next to him, "that I am damned hungry!"

"So am I!" his friend replied, "and certainly thirsty!
Would you like to know what there is to eat?"

"I cannot see a menu," the Earl remarked.

His companion drew a piece of paper from his
pocket.

"I got this from the Caterers," he said. "I thought it would be amusing to keep to show my sons and grand-sons how greedy we were on this auspicious occasion."

The Earl laughed and looked at the list.

160   tureens of soup, 160 dishes of fish;
160   hot joints, 160 dishes of vegetables;
480   sauce boats (lobster, butter, mint);
 80   dishes braised ham, 80 savoury pies;
 80   dishes of goose, 80 of savoury cakes;
 80   of braised beef, 80 braised capons;
1,190   side dishes;
320   dishes of mounted pastry, 320 of small pastry;
400   dishes of jellies and creams;
160   dishes of shellfish (lobster and crayfish);
160   dishes of cold roast fowl, 80 of cold lamb.

"If we eat all that," the Earl exclaimed when he had read it, "it is doubtful if we shall be able to waddle home!"

"The people I am sorry for are the Peeresses," his friend replied.

"Of course!" the Earl replied. "I forgot they would get nothing, they must be starving!"

He looked up at the Galleries as he spoke and saw the ladies in their glittering jewels looking down at them.

He was aware that Imogen was trying to catch his eye and deliberately inspected the opposite side of the Hall.

"I will tell you what I am going to do," his friend went on. "I am going to put some cold chicken in a handkerchief and throw it up to my son. I hope he has the good sense to share it with my wife; other-wise I shall get a cold shoulder when I return home!"

The Earl was relieved when the Banquet was over and he could return in his ornate State Coach,

which had been in the family for over a century, to
Meltham House.

There he found he had plenty of time to have a
bath, change, and be ready for his guests, who were
invited for ten o'clock.

Fireworks were exploding in Hyde Park, rockets
whistling into the sky, Church bells ringing, and guns
thundering as the Earl's guests began to arrive at Meltham House; many of them still in the elaborate gowns
and the glittering tiaras they had worn in the Abbey.

Among the first to arrive, as the Earl had expected,
was Lady Imogen.

She was wearing a very fine necklace of emeralds
which the Earl had given to her during the first weeks
of their wild infatuation with each other.

A tiara of the same jewel glittered in her hair and
she immediately informed the Earl that she had bor-
rowed it for the occasion and wished more than anything else in the world to possess it.

She looked up at him with an expression in her
green eyes which was a provocative invitation.

At the same time he had the feeling that she was
calculating how far she could press him into making
their association legal.

He greeted her with courtesy and when she held
on to his hand longer than was necessary, freed himself to welcome the next guest who followed her into
the large Salon which had been decorated with an
amazing display of lilies.

Beyond the Salon, the windows of the Ball-Room
opened onto the garden where fountains were lit
by different coloured lights, and Chinese lanterns hung
from the trees.

The paths were edged with fairy lights and there
were specially constructed little arbours made comfortable with sofas and soft cushions, where those who
found the dancing too strenuous could flirt half
screened by fragrant flowers.

A thousand candles lit the glittering chandeliers in

the Ball-Room and in honour of the occasion the dec-
orations were all in red, white, and blue.

The Earl was known to be very fastidious about
his friends and an invitation to Meltham House was
more sought after than one to Carlton House.

Only the most important, intelligent, and amusing
of the *Beau Monde* had been asked this evening.

The guests were well aware that of all the parties
being given in London that evening after the King's
Coronation, an invitation from the Earl was the most
prized.

The Earl was irritated to find that as he greeted
his guests, Lady Imogen stood so near to him that it
almost appeared as if she were receiving them with
him.

It was quite obvious that she intended to make it
very clear to everyone arriving at Meltham House
that she had a special place there.

It was, he thought, what he might have expected
her to do.

At the same time, the fact that she was deliberately
inviting comment about their association annoyed
him.

More and more guests arrived and by half past ten
he was aware that he was watching the door in an
apprehensive fashion which was very unlike his usual
air of indifference.

Then, just as he was beginning to wonder if anything untoward had happened to delay her, Celesta
appeared.

The Earl had sent a carriage for her and Giles, and
the fact that they were late was not Celesta's fault,
but her brother's.

When Giles had arrived back from the Fleet Prison
in the carriage that the Earl had provided for him,
Celesta had been glad that he had thought to stop at
his lodgings to collect his trunks.

He had made no effort to tidy himself, shave, or
put on a fresh cravat since she and Nana had left
him in prison.

He was in fact extremely drunk and Celesta knew when the carriage drew up at the Garden Cottage it was only because it had taken nearly two hours to travel down from London that he was not incapable.

On arrival he immediately asked for a drink and when Nana informed him firmly and with truth that there was nothing alcoholic in the house, he swore and, staggering upstairs, pulled off his dirty, stained clothes and got into bed.

He slept until noon. Then Nana persuaded him to eat a sensible meal and to rest while she pressed his best clothes preparatory for the evening.

"Why the hell do we have to go to a Ball?" Giles asked Celesta when she went to see him in his bedroom after luncheon.

"His Lordship asked that we should attend the party he is giving after the Coronation," Celesta replied.

"Well, you can go without me," Giles answered fretfully.

"I cannot do that," Celesta said. "To begin with, I cannot go alone, and secondly it was only on condition that we attended his party that the Earl paid your debts."

"Did he say so?" Giles asked.

"Yes," Celesta answered, "and you do see, Giles, that we must be very agreeable to him; for without his generosity you would still be in that terrible prison."

"I expect Crawthorne would have paid up if you had dined with him as he asked you to do."

"He wanted me to go alone," Celesta said, "and, Giles, he is an evil man. I am sure of it. You cannot wish me to have anything to do with a man . . . like that!"

"Nonsense!" Giles said, "Crawthorne is all right. In fact no-one can be more amusing or a better host when he wishes to be!"

"He did not seem very anxious to pay your debts," Celesta answered coolly, "and what is more, at first he said he could not afford to do so."

Giles appeared to have no answer to this, but after a moment he said:

"Well, as Meltham has coughed up, there is no need to worry as to who pays them. I cannot think why the hell he wants me to go poodle-faking. If I had enough money I would go to my Club."

Celesta clasped her hands together.

"Oh, Giles, do not go gaming again! Surely you have learnt by this time that you cannot win, and besides the extra money the Earl gave you was not meant to be thrown away at cards."

She paused to say firmly:

"Before you spend one penny of that money you must pay back Nana what she spent yesterday. A pound for the runner who brought your note and it was two pounds of her money that we brought to the prison."

"I shall want everything I have got," Giles said in a surly voice.

"You are going to pay Nana," Celesta replied.

"Oh, very well. Take the money yourself! It is lying on the dressing-table," Giles said. "But if you think I am going to stay in this benighted hole with you nagging at me, you are very much mistaken!"

He was in a disagreeable mood for the rest of the afternoon. Celesta was wise enough to know that it was the result of the drink he had consumed the day before and left him alone.

Only when it was time to go to London did Celesta and Nana have difficulty in persuading Giles to dress.

Having spoilt six cravats before he could tie one to his liking, he had kept the carriage for over half an hour.

Finally they set off.

For the first time it seemed to Celesta that Giles grew more cheerful.

"At least I shall get something to drink at Meltham's," he said.

"Giles! Please be careful. Do not drink too much," Celesta pleaded. "You know how ashamed I should feel if you were anything but sober, and you look so smart. I am so proud of you at the moment."

She flattered and cajoled him all the way to London, and when finally they stepped out at Meltham House he was, she thought with relief, in a surprisingly good humour.

Despite his disagreeableness about attending the Earl's party, Celesta thought secretly that he was rather pleased at the thought of being a guest at Meltham House and was well aware that only the élite of Society would be present.

Celesta had been so concerned for Giles that she had hardly had time to worry about herself.

She had hated the thought of wearing the gown her mother had sent her and yet, when finally she had it on, she knew that she had never before worn anything so beautiful.

Her mother had not only sent her the gown from France but she had enclosed with it a small corset that had been introduced the previous year when the straight Empire gowns first designed for the Empress Josephine had finally gone out of fashion.

Celesta had no idea until this moment how tiny her waist could be or how perfect her figure.

The frills of lace, the bunches of camelias, and the expensive perfection of the gauze and satin were a perfect frame for the whiteness of her skin and the soft gold of her hair.

She looked incredibly lovely as she and Giles entered the Salon.

She stood for a moment in the doorway, her eyes wide and a little apprehensive, the light from the candles revealing the sensitivity of her curved lips and the perfection of her features.

"I was afraid that something had delayed you," the Earl said in his deep voice.

He felt Celesta's fingers flutter in his and knew she was nervous.

She swept him a curtsy, then as she rose he still kept hold of her hand.

"Now that you are here," he said, "I want you to open my Ball with me, because this is not only my party, Celesta, but also yours."

"Mine?" she asked in a very small voice.

"Your first Ball," he said, "and I am very honoured that I can be instrumental in introducing anything so lovely to the Social World."

What he said was perfectly audible to a number of people who had been standing round talking before Celesta's entrance.

There was a silence after he had spoken, then after greeting Giles the Earl led both Celesta and her brother through the Salon and into the Ball-Room.

A number of older guests had already seated themselves on the gold chairs round the room while others were standing at the open windows looking out at the fountains in the garden.

The Band was playing softly but no-one had as yet begun to dance.

The Earl smiled at Celesta.

"Will you honour me with this waltz?" he asked.

"I . . . I am afraid I . . . may not be . . . good enough," she replied in a voice that only he could hear.

"I think you will find that our steps will match each other perfectly," he replied.

He put his arm round her waist and drew her onto the floor.

She was very light and although she was afraid of making mistakes she found it was surprisingly easy to follow the Earl's lead.

There was something reassuring in the firmness of his arm round her waist and with her hand in his she felt that she need have no thought for herself, but just leave everything to him.

They moved round the floor and danced alone for at least a minute before they were joined by other couples.

The Earl knew that everybody's eyes in the Ball-

Room were on them and they were all speculating as to who Celesta might be.

He had wanted to find a way of making it quite clear that Lady Imogen was not the only woman in his life.

He had contrived it in a manner that would ensure, as he well knew, that for the rest of the evening and tomorrow, the gossiping tongues of the *Beau Monde* would talk only of Celesta.

"Is it what you expected?" he asked softly.

"Much, much more marvellous!" she answered, "but will . . . people not think it . . . strange that you invited me?"

"One reason is quite obvious," he answered.

"What is . . . that?"

"That you are very beautiful."

Celesta blushed and dropped her eyes.

"If you do not smile at me," he said, "those watching will think I am not saying the pleasant things that you would want to hear."

She looked up, saw the twinkle in his eyes, and laughed.

"That is better!" he approved.

"You sound as if you are producing me . . . like an actress."

"Perhaps I am."

"But . . . why?"

"One day I will tell you—but not at this moment."

Celesta glanced round.

"Your house . . . this room . . . it is a perfect stage for . . . you."

"And you?"

"I am only a strolling player."

"Tonight you are the leading lady!"

"And when the curtain . . . falls?"

"What happens afterwards will be entirely your decision."

Celesta felt that everything they said to each other had a deeper meaning than the actual words they spoke.

She could not explain it even to herself, but it was part of the strange bewilderment, almost an enchantment, that had enveloped her ever since the Earl had kissed her.

It was like moving in a dream and she could not believe that everything which was happening to her was real.

"You are like a flower!" the Earl said softly as they moved to a slow waltz.

"Flowers wither and die . . . and are then . . . forgotten."

"I was wrong—you are not a flower but a star—unforgettable and for the moment out of reach."

"It sounds . . . distant and rather . . . cold."

"Then again I have made a mistake because your lips were warm."

Celesta blushed again and in her confusion missed a step.

"You are making me . . . stumble," she murmured.

"I will take care of you," he said quietly and his arm tightened round her waist.

They danced for a long time.

Then the Earl introduced her to a number of elegantly gowned and slightly older women who had been watching their performance on the dance floor.

As he had predicted, they were all charming but obviously curious as to who Celesta might be, until one of them remarked:

"But of course! I knew your mother!"

Celesta stiffened, expecting an insult, but the lady continued:

"We were girls together and I shall never forget how lovely Elaine was. When we attended the same Balls all the men clustered round her and the rest of us had to be content with the partners she did not want!"

There was a little laugh and then the lady added:

"You are very like her, my dear, and I am sure your success will be as phenomenal as hers."

The Earl introduced her to so many people that

Celesta gave up trying to remember their names or even what he told her about them.

When she met the Earl's men-friends they all asked her to dance.

She had so many partners and they paid her so many compliments that the hours seemed to speed by.

"Where have you been?"

"Why haven't we met before?"

"How can you have hidden yourself away until now?"

She answered the same questions over and over again but her eyes shone and her lips were smiling.

Then in the early hours of the morning she found herself standing in the garden with Giles.

"It is a wonderful party!" she cried. "I never knew that I could enjoy myself so much!"

"I would be enjoying it more," Giles replied, "if I did not keep remembering I have to go back to the country."

"It may not be for long," Celesta said consolingly. "We have not had time to talk about things yet, Giles, but I am sure there is something you can do to make money."

"The only way of making money," Giles replied, "is by gaming, and I would not get far on the pittance I have in my pocket at the moment."

"Please do not throw it away," Celesta said quickly. "I was thinking that perhaps you could find . . . work of some sort."

"Work?" Giles ejaculated. "What the devil do you think I could do?"

"I feel there must be something," Celesta said, "but do not let us talk of it now, Giles, I am so happy. It is so marvellous to be here."

"And I was very surprised to learn of your where-abouts."

Celesta turned round sharply.

She could not mistake that voice with an under-tone of evil in it.

Standing beside them was Lord Crawthorne!

Celesta did not speak and he added:

"When someone told me at the Club that the most beautiful girl at Meltham House this evening was Miss Celesta Wroxley, I had to come and find out why you spurned my invitation to dinner last night."

Celesta glanced at Giles. He was looking at Lord Crawthorne with a frown on his face.

"Giles, my dear boy," Lord Crawthorne said with an appearance of affability, "I had made arrangements to come to the Fleet Prison this morning and bail you out. Your sister told me of your unfortunate predicament."

"You must have had my letters," Giles said sourly.

"Letters?" Lord Crawthorne exclaimed. "What letters?"

"I wrote to you three times."

"If you did, I never received them."

Celesta was quite sure that Lord Crawthorne was lying, but it was something neither she nor Giles could prove.

She put her hand on her brother's arm.

"Please, Giles. I must go back into the Ball-Room. My partner will be waiting for me."

"One moment!" Lord Crawthorne said. "Giles, I have something of great importance to tell your sister—something which will be of benefit to you both, so I know you will understand if I say that I wish to speak to her alone."

"No!" Celesta said quickly. "No, Giles! Do not leave me!"

But already her brother had turned away.

"If you think I want to talk to you—you are mistaken!" he said to Lord Crawthorne.

And before she could prevent him he walked away towards the house.

Celesta would have followed but Lord Crawthorne caught hold of her wrist.

"I really have something of import to say to you, Celesta," he said.

She tried to pull her hand away but it was impossible.

Relentlessly he drew her towards an arbour which was just a little to the left of them.

She still struggled to free herself from his hold.

But there were people moving about the garden and she thought how embarrassing it would be if they should see her struggling with Lord Crawthorne.

What would the Earl think if she behaved in a manner which drew attention to herself?

Because there was nothing else she could do, she was forced to let Lord Crawthorne lead her into the arbour. On reaching it she sat down on the very edge of the seat.

"I cannot stay long, My Lord," she said nervously, "otherwise my partner will come in search of me."

He turned sideways to look at her, his arm outstretched along the seat behind her back.

"I was very disappointed you would not dine with me last night," he said. "Did Meltham release your brother?"

"His Lordship was very kind," Celesta replied defiantly.

She saw a sudden expression on Lord Crawthorne's face which she realised was one of hatred, but he merely said in his silky voice that made her tremble:

"I would have been—kind too!"

"You made it quite clear, My Lord, that you could not afford to effect Giles's release."

"I did not say that I would not do so," Lord Crawthorne answered. "It might have been an inconvenience to find so much money at a moment's notice, but if you had asked me prettily, as I had the feeling you might do, then as I have already said, Giles would have been a free man."

"He is free now!" Celesta said, "and I think there is little point in our discussing the matter any further. I must return to the Ball, My Lord."

She would have risen but once again his hand went out to hold on to her.

"You are very lovely," he said and there was a note in his voice which made her tremble.

"Let me go!"

"That is something I do not intend to do," Lord Crawthorne said, "either now or in the future."

"I do not understand what you are trying to say."

"I think you do," he answered. "You are fond of your brother, and I promise you I can make Giles happy and re-instate him in the life he likes, if you will be a little more amenable and understand how much we can mean to each other."

"We can mean . . . nothing to each . . . other!" Celesta said in a voice which she hoped sounded strong and firm, but which in fact was weak and frightened.

"There is so much I can give you."

Lord Crawthorne's arm went round her waist as he spoke and he pulled her towards him.

Celesta gave a little cry and put her hands against his chest.

"Do not touch me!" she cried.

Then as she realised he was about to kiss her, she turned her face away so that his lips touched only her cheek.

The mere touch was enough!

All her revulsion and disgust for Lord Crawthorne came flooding over her, inciting her to a panic that gave her a strength she did not know she possessed.

She fought herself free of him and even as he clutched at her, ran from the arbour.

Then as she was wildly running to escape there was a man standing in her way and she bumped into him.

She knew before she touched him who it was and felt an inexplicable relief.

"I was looking for you," the Earl said.

Because she was feeling so afraid, Celesta put out her hands to hold on to him.

He could see by the sharpening of her features and the darkness of her eyes that she was upset.

"What has happened?" he asked quickly.

Then he saw who followed her.

Lord Crawthorne in his haste to prevent Celesta escaping from him had also come from the arbour without looking where he was going.

Now he found himself face to face with the Earl and there was no disguising the fact that he was disconcerted.

The light from a Chinese lantern hanging from the bough of a tree directly above them revealed the expression on his face.

"This is a surprise, Crawthorne!" the Earl said in a voice that was insulting merely because he drawled the words. "I arranged my list of guests with great care and your name was not on it!"

"I came with Lord Walten," Lord Crawthorne answered. "He left his wife here earlier in the evening and promised to collect her. He had no carriage and I obliged him with a seat in mine."

"Then I suggest you wait for him outside," the Earl drawled, "with the other lackeys!"

"Are you turning me from your house, Meltham?" Lord Crawthorne asked in a tone of fury.

"If you do not leave at once, I will have you thrown out," the Earl replied. "I promise you I am not speaking lightly."

For a moment it seemed that Lord Crawthorne would defy him.

Then, as if he realised that the Earl would have no hesitation in putting his threat into action, he made an inarticulate sound of repressed fury and walked away.

The Earl waited until he was out of ear-shot and then he looked down at Celesta.

She was standing close against him, her hands against his chest as if she felt without support she would fall to the ground.

"It is all right now, Celesta," he said. "Why were you with him?"

"I could not help it," she answered in a low voice.

"He dragged me into the arbour and I did not wish to make a scene at your party."

"Nor did I," the Earl agreed, "otherwise I would have knocked him down. I told you to have nothing to do with him."

"He . . . frightens me," Celesta said, "but now that Giles is incensed with him there is no reason why I should ever see him again."

She spoke in a low voice as if she would convince herself.

"You must come back to the Ball," the Earl said. "Everyone is talking of your attraction and exclaiming about your beauty!"

Celesta raised her head to look at him and he felt there was a question in her eyes.

"It is true!"

He smiled at her.

"Come!" he said, "I think it is time you had some supper and even after the enormous meal I ate in Westminster Hall I could still enjoy a glass of wine."

The Supper-Room was arranged with small tables on each of which there was a lighted candle surrounded by a circle of roses.

Celesta, who had had nothing to eat since they'd left the Cottage, where she and Giles had enjoyed only a very light dinner prepared by Nana, found the dishes the Earl recommended for her attention both exciting and delicious.

"I have never eaten quail before," she exclaimed.

The Earl sent for lobster, oysters, and stuffed chickens to tempt her appetite, but she could eat only a little.

He also persuaded her to have a glass of champagne.

"This too is something I have never tasted before," she told him.

She thought he seemed pleased that he could produce so many new delights to entertain her.

"Have you enjoyed yourself?" he asked.

"It has been . . . wonderful . . . so different from

what I expected a Ball to be like," Celesta answered, "and everyone has been very kind."

"I told you they would be," the Earl said.

"You were right, although I admit I did not believe you," Celesta answered.

She gave a little sigh.

"Now it is time for me to go home."

"There are so many more things I would like to say to you," the Earl said.

There was a note in his voice that made her eyes fall before his.

"Do not be afraid," he said quickly. "I am not going to plague you with questions or decisions tonight. I want you to be happy. I want you to appreciate how lovely you are and to find that life, when you are not hating anyone, can be very enjoyable."

"It has all been . . . marvellous!" Celesta said and her eyes met his.

She did not know why, but suddenly it was hard to breathe.

She felt as if he held her spellbound.

He was not touching her and yet she felt his arms were round her and his lips were seeking hers as they had done before.

Again that strange feeling she had felt within her breast when he had kissed her yesterday seemed to sweep over her in a tidal wave, warm, insidious, and incomprehensible.

She could not escape; could not break away; she did not even want to do so.

Then abruptly a voice shattered the spell.

"So this is where you are, Vidal!" Lady Imogen exclaimed.

Her voice was hard and the expression on her face was one of barely suppressed anger.

She was escorted by three young men and as the Earl rose slowly to his feet they looked uncomfortable, as if they sensed there might be a scene.

"I was waiting for you to take me down to supper," Lady Imogen said.

Because she was angry her voice seemed to ring out in the Supper-Room so that a number of people at adjacent tables turned their heads to see what was happening.

"I must apologise if you waited for me," the Earl replied. "But as you must have realised, Imogen, it was my duty to take my most important guest down to supper, and that of course is Miss Wroxley!"

For a moment Lady Imogen went pale with anger.

Then before she could speak, before the words of fury which trembled on her lips could find expression, the Earl turned to Celesta.

Putting his hand out to assist her to rise, he said conversationally:

"We must find your brother. He will be wishing to escort you home."

Without even a look in Lady Imogen's direction, the Earl manoeuvred Celesta past the three young men and they walked across the crowded Supper-Room followed by speculative and extremely interested glances from all those present.

They reached the Salon in which the Earl had received his guests.

It was empty because most people were either in the Ball-Room or having supper.

"I think as you have a long drive ahead of you that it would be wise for you to go now," the Earl said quietly.

"I am sorry if I have caused you any . . . trouble," Celesta said.

"You have caused me no trouble," the Earl answered. "You have been everything I expected you to be, and more."

"It has been very wonderful!" she murmured.

The Earl told a footman to find Sir Giles Wroxley, who, being found at a bar in the Dining-Room, appeared in a few seconds.

Celesta knew at once that he had been drinking; he was walking with the deliberate care of a man who is aware that he is unsteady on his feet.

The carriage was brought to the door and the Earl saw them into it.

"I shall be coming to the Priory very shortly," he said quietly and stepped back as the horses started off.

Giles hardly spoke but settled himself in a corner of the carriage where very soon he fell asleep.

Celesta looked out into the darkness.

It seemed to her the music of the Band was still playing in her ears and she could feel her feet still dancing over the polished floor.

She had no idea that a Ball could be so gay, so exciting, or that men would say such fascinating and complimentary things to her.

She tried not to think about Lord Crawthorne and what she had felt when he had attempted to kiss her.

Instead she remembered how she had danced with the Earl; how easy it had been to follow his steps.

Her thoughts brought her to the moment when they had looked into each other's eyes at the supper-table.

It had seemed as if he was telling her something very special, something she longed to hear.

'He is different . . . very different from other men,' Celesta thought.

She wondered why it was an obscure pain that every mile she drove took her further away from him.

Chapter Six

Celesta was in the Sitting-Room with Giles trying to coax him into a better temper.

She realised he had not completely slept off the amount of drink he had consumed the night before and she looked with consternation at the dark lines under his eyes.

He appeared much older than he should have, and there was no doubt, she thought, that his character had changed since he had lived in London.

It was difficult to realise that he was the same gay, delightful brother whom she had loved as a child.

Now, because through his own fault he had thrown away his possessions, Giles was prepared to snarl at and dislike everyone with whom he came in contact.

"You must have enjoyed yourself last night," Celesta insisted.

As she spoke she remembered what a fascinating, enchanted evening it had been for her.

"Enjoy myself?" Giles questioned. "Do you think I can enjoy myself when I see how much money Meltham can afford to expend on one Ball? Why should he have a house like that and everything he requires in life while I barely have two coins to rub together in my pocket?"

"You had more than that after Papa died," Celesta said quietly.

"Throw it in my face that I have been a fool!" Giles exclaimed angrily.

He paused for a moment to add in a surly manner:

"It was Meltham's fault! If he had not interfered I am certain I should have won that hand."

"Whether you were playing against the Earl or any-one else," Celesta said, "surely the cards you held would have been the same?"

This was irrefutable, and Giles lapsed into sulky silence.

"I must have some money," he said after a little while, "and what is more immediate, I want a drink!"

"There is nothing in the house," Celesta answered. "As you well know, we cannot afford any sort of wine."

"Oh, my God!" Giles ejaculated, "was ever a man bedevilled by bad fortune and forced into a worse situation than this?"

"At least you are not in prison!" Celesta reminded him.

"At least I could get a drink in the Fleet if I had the money," Giles retorted.

Celesta rose from the stool on which she had been sitting.

There was no point in arguing, she thought, no point in trying to convince Giles that he might have been in worse circumstances than he was at the moment.

At least he had a roof over his head, though it was difficult not to keep remembering that, except for his wild gaming, the Priory would still be theirs.

She found herself thinking how it might have been possible to sell the Cottage or a few acres of land instead of losing the whole Estate.

She heard the sound of wheels outside and walking to the window saw a carriage drawn by two horses with two liveried attendants on the box pull up out-side the Cottage.

She thought it might be the Earl and felt a sudden leap of excitement in her heart.

Then as the footmen jumped down to open the door she saw inside the carriage the dissipated lined face of Lord Crawthorne.

She turned hastily towards Giles, who was sunk in an arm-chair, his feet stretched out in front of him.

"Lord Crawthorne is here!"

"Here?" Giles asked in surprise.

Then he said harshly with an unpleasant twist of his lips:

"I wonder why he could not keep away?"

"I do not want to see him," Celesta cried.

She ran across the room and up the narrow staircase just as Nana crossed the small Hall to answer the rattat of His Lordship's footman, which echoed round the Cottage.

Celesta had not told her brother how the Earl had ordered Lord Crawthorne from the Ball last night.

Neither had she related to him the way in which Lord Crawthorne had tried to kiss her.

She was not certain what Giles's reaction might have been.

Admittedly he had walked away rudely when Lord Crawthorne appeared, but it was hard to believe that what had amounted almost to an adoration of his friend could have changed so quickly into what appeared to be dislike.

"One never knows with Giles," Celesta told herself. "His feelings change from one minute to the next!"

It was true that since he had been home Giles's attitude towards herself and Nana had been one of disagreeableness.

Yet they both knew him well enough to know that he could alter in the flicker of an eye-lid and exude a charm which would make them run round only too willing to wait on him.

From the top of the stairs Celesta heard the front door open and then Lord Crawthorne's suave voice say:

"I am Lord Crawthorne. I have called to see Miss Celesta Wroxley!"

"I'll tell her, M'Lord. Will you come in?"

"Thank you."

"I think Sir Giles and Miss Celesta are in the Sitting-Room, M'Lord."

Nana led the way and opened the door which Celes-

ta had shut behind her, but when Lord Crawthorne
entered the room Nana left it ajar.

"Well, Giles," Celesta heard Lord Crawthorne say
in his most affable tone, "I hope you are pleased to
see me."

"What do you want?"

"As it happens," Lord Crawthorne replied, "I come
bearing gifts."

Giles did not answer and he went on:

"A gift which you will certainly appreciate, my dear
boy, unless I am very much mistaken."

"What is it?"

Giles's tone sounded surly but Celesta could hear
the curiosity in it.

"A dozen bottles of a really fine French Brandy and
another dozen of a superlative claret!"

There was silence for a moment, then Giles said in
a very different tone:

"You are a Trojan! If you only knew how I have
been thirsting for a decent drink!"

"Then there is no need, my dear boy, for you to
thirst any longer! Tell my footman to bring it in."

Giles pulled open the Sitting-Room door.

"Nana!" he shouted. "Bring me some glasses!"

Then he crossed the Hall.

The footman was already carrying a case of brandy
up the small flagged path.

Giles waited while it was set down in the Hall,
then he picked up a bottle and carried it back to the
Sitting-Room.

"This is the real stuff!" Celesta heard him say. "I
can't describe the muck I had to drink in the Fleet!"

"I must tell you how much I regret the misunder-
standing which caused you to be so long in that unpleasant place," Lord Crawthorne said.

Giles did not answer and Celesta was sure he was
busy opening the bottle.

Nana carried two cut-crystal glasses into the
Sitting-Room on a silver salver. She re-crossed the Hall
with a disapproving expression on her face.

"You will join me?" Celesta heard Giles say.

There was the sound of liquid being poured into a glass.

"Of course!" Lord Crawthorne answered. "I wish to drink your health, dear boy, and when you are feeling a little more amenable I have something of great import to tell you."

"What is that?" Giles asked.

"I think I have discovered a way in which you can get back the Priory and your Estate."

"Are you still suggesting I should buy it?" Giles asked. "I have exactly five pounds in my pocket, which is all that stands between me and starvation!"

"I have a much better plan," Lord Crawthorne said. "But before we talk of such serious matters, let me enquire as to the health of your most entrancing sister."

"Celesta is all right!" Giles said impatiently.

"Although I was of course anxious to see you," Lord Crawthorne continued, "I was also consumed by a most urgent desire to continue my conversation with your sister where it left off last night."

"What happened?" Giles asked.

"I was threatened by our host and turned out of his house!"

"Good God! And you allowed him to behave like that to you?"

"I had little choice at the time, but I promise you, Giles, that I do not accept insults such as that easily."

Lord Crawthorne's voice was sinister as he went on:

"Nor do I allow the same man to trick me, as Meltham has tricked me, or insult me, as Meltham has insulted me not once but twice!"

"What will you do about it?" Giles asked. "As you can well suppose, when I think of him sitting in my house and riding over my land, I loathe the swine!"

"That is just what I hoped you would say," Lord Crawthorne answered. "So, Giles, let us put out heads together. I have a plan which I feel sure will meet with your approval."

"Tell me what it is," Giles said eagerly, "but first let me get you another drink."

"I want no more," Lord Crawthorne replied. "It is too early in the morning, but you go ahead, dear boy, I brought it for you."

There was a pause while Celesta was certain that Giles was re-filling his glass. Then Lord Crawthorne said:

"I suggest you shut the door. It would be a mistake for anyone to over-hear what I have to tell you."

The door was closed.

Celesta went into her bed-room.

What plan did Lord Crawthorne have which could possibly restore the Priory to Giles and give him back the Estates which were now legally owned by the Earl?

Whatever the idea was, she was certain it was wrong, if not wicked.

There had been something horrible in the slimy notes of Lord Crawthorne's voice as he spoke.

She could understand his being incensed and in-sulted by the way the Earl had spoken to him last night.

At the same time he was entirely in the wrong in appearing uninvited at Meltham House. He should have known quite well that the Earl was not the sort of person who would tolerate an intruder.

"He is plotting some terrible mischief!" Celesta told herself, "and Giles will be involved in it."

She put her fingers to her forehead trying to think.

She must find out what he was suggesting, because she was certain that he intended to harm the Earl.

It seemed impossible that he could do him serious damage. Yet she knew that she would fight in every way in her power to prevent a man so evil and so de-graded as Lord Crawthorne from injuring the Earl, even if it only affected his pocket.

However, only to think of the Earl was to know his strength, his impregnable position in Society, and to remember he was a very close friend of the King.

How could anyone as debauched as Lord Crawthorne attempt anything that would not make him a laughing-stock in the social world?

At the same time Celesta felt apprehensive.

She could not bear to think that Giles, who had been a recipient of the Earl's generosity, should be ready to intrigue against him with a man who had proven himself completely indifferent to his sufferings in prison.

"How can Giles be such a fool as to trust him again?" Celesta asked.

She was ashamed that her brother could change his attitude so easily simply because Lord Crawthorne had supplied him with the drink he craved.

"What am I to do?" Celesta asked, and could find no answer to her own question.

It was getting near luncheon-time and Nana came up the stairs.

"Do you think His Lordship'll be staying for a meal?" she asked anxiously.

"I cannot imagine he wishes to eat with us," Celesta answered. "What have we for luncheon today?"

"Only a brace of pigeons," Nana answered. "Mr. Copple brought them for me this morning when he delivered your newspaper. And very grateful I was to him."

Celesta laughed.

"I think, Nana, Mr. Copple is courting you!"

"Get along with you!" Nana replied. "It's just that he enjoys a gossip about old times and there's no-one else in the village as has the time to waste on him."

"Whatever his motives," Celesta said, "we are delighted with the pigeons. That will be one for Giles and one for His Lordship, if he stays. And you can give me an egg."

"It's not right that someone who can have everything should eat the little we've got," Nana said crossly. "And bringing Master Giles all that spirit! You know it's bad for him!"

"I do indeed, Nana," Celesta agreed. "Let us hope

that Lord Crawthorne goes back to London quickly.
I cannot bear to know he is here in the Cottage."

Even as she spoke she felt it was a forlorn hope and
sure enough a few minutes later she heard Giles
shouting to Nana that His Lordship was staying to
luncheon.

Then he was calling her name.

"Celesta! Come downstairs! I want you!"

There was nothing Celesta could do but obey.

Slowly, wishing she could make some excuse to stay
in her room, she descended the stairs and walked into
the Sitting-Room.

It seemed to her that Lord Crawthorne was looking
more repulsive than he had the night before.

There were dark bags under his eyes and the deep
lines running from his nose to his chin made him seem
more than usually sardonic, or perhaps it was because
in the bright sunlight he seemed to have an unnatural
pallor.

"I am at your feet, Celesta!" he said and lifted her
hand to his lips.

Once again she felt herself repelled by the touch of
his mouth on her skin.

Without looking at him directly she was aware that
his eyes were flickering over her, making her feel as
if he mentally undressed her.

"I have brought you a present," he went on.

"I have read that one should beware of the Greeks
when they come bearing gifts!" Celesta replied. "And
that goes for Londoners."

Lord Crawthorne merely laughed as if she had said
something witty and drawing a case from his pocket
placed it in her hands.

It was a velvet case and when she opened it she
saw to her astonishment that inside was a diamond
bracelet.

She looked at it for a moment, then shut the case
and handed it back to him.

"It is kind of Your Lordship," she said, "but I never

accept presents of that sort from anyone but my immediate family."

"I am a very old friend of your brother's," Lord Crawthorne said.

"But still no relation," Celesta insisted, "and therefore, My Lord, I must refuse your gift."

Lord Crawthorne turned to Giles.

"Help me, Giles!" he said. "Your sister is refusing what is only a small tribute to her beauty."

Celesta glanced sharply at her brother.

She was afraid that he might try to force her to accept Lord Crawthorne's present simply because it was valuable.

She saw that Giles was looking at Lord Crawthorne with a strange expression on his face and one which appeared to her to be calculating.

Then he said slowly as if he deliberated the words:

"My sister is right, My Lord. A young lady in her position could not possibly accept anything so valuable, whatever the reason for it being offered."

Giles accentuated the last words and Celesta knew that Lord Crawthorne glanced at him in surprise.

Then before anything more could be said Nana announced luncheon.

Lord Crawthorne ate the pigeon which was tender and well cooked.

Celesta had the feeling that it was of no particular concern to him what he consumed.

Giles sat at the top of the table with Lord Crawthorne on his right and Celesta on his left, and she was aware that all through the meal His Lordship's eyes hardly left her face.

It was difficult for her to appear unconcerned when she knew that every nerve in her body shrank from the expression with which he regarded her.

Celesta was very innocent.

At the same time her experience with Lord Crawthorne both at his house and at the Ball had made her aware that the lust he had for her emanated from him like some poison from which she must escape.

Giles, who had been drinking glass after glass of brandy, made the meal an opportunity for a long harangue against the Earl because he now owned the Priory.

"What does it matter to someone like that that the whole history of our family lies within its walls?" he asked. "The rich crush those who are weaker, stamp on the faces of ordinary people, and when it comes to a War, expect other men to fight so that they can save their own skins!"

As Giles had never been in the Army, nor had he ever fought for anyone save himself, Celesta could not help thinking that this was unfair.

However she knew by now that when Giles had reached the state of being voluble any opposition to what he was saying merely antagonised him to fury and he was past listening to logic.

She therefore remained silent and so did Lord Crawthorne.

He appeared quite uninterested in Giles and what he was saying.

Nana had made a peach tart which Lord Crawthorne ate without comment. Giles refused it.

When Celesta had finished she rose to her feet.

"I am afraid there is no port, My Lord," she said, "perhaps you would like a glass of your own claret, in which case I will leave you and Giles alone."

"There is no need for you to go," he said quickly.

"I must behave with propriety," Celesta replied with a faint smile.

"In which case," Lord Crawthorne answered, "I will drink my claret in the Sitting-Room with you."

Celesta glanced nervously at her brother.

"Will you come with us, Giles?" she asked.

"Yes, of course."

Giles rose from the table to follow Celesta into the Sitting-Room.

"I am sure, dear boy," Lord Crawthorne said, "you will understand if I tell you that I would like to talk with your sister alone?"

"No! No!" Celesta said quickly.

To her utter astonishment Giles replied:

"Celesta must be chaperoned. I am sure my father, had he been alive, would not have left her alone with you, or with any other man."

Celesta was so surprised that she could only stare at Giles.

He threw himself down in an arm-chair in a manner which made it quite obvious that he had no intention of complying with Lord Crawthorne's request.

For a moment she thought with amusement that His Lordship was disconcerted and there was an expression of anger on his face.

Before he could say anything Celesta interposed:

"I am sure that you and Giles, My Lord, have a great many things to discuss and you will therefore excuse me if I bid you good-bye."

She curtsied and before Lord Crawthorne could touch her hand she slipped from the room, closing the door behind her.

She went into the kitchen to find Nana washing up the dishes they had used at luncheon.

"Has he gone?" Nana asked.

"No, unfortunately," Celesta replied. "Nana, you will never believe it, but he wanted to speak to me alone and Giles refused to allow it, saying that Papa would have wanted me to be chaperoned!"

Nana put down the plate she was drying with a murmur of satisfaction.

"There!" she said. "I knew there was still good in Master Giles. It's just that he's been led astray by his smart London friends."

"I have never known Giles to do anything like that before," Celesta said. "Perhaps, after all, Nana, he does care for me a little?"

"I'm sure he does!" Nana said, "and let's hope those so-called friends of his will leave him alone. Bringing down all that drink! It's the last thing he should have!"

"He has drunk over half a bottle already!" Celesta said. "If only we could hide the rest!"

They both sighed, knowing that they dare not interfere with Giles's drinking when it meant so much to
him.

Celesta helped Nana with the washing-up, then
went upstairs to her bed-room.

She would have liked to go for a walk in the sunshine, but she was afraid lest Lord Crawthorne should
see her go and follow so that he would be alone with
her.

She suddenly felt so much happier and less afraid
than she had been since Lord Crawthorne's arrival.

If Giles was going to behave towards her in the way
he should, then it was obvious things would be far
better than they had been in the past.

The Earl said she should be chaperoned and he had
been right!

Celesta felt how unpleasant it would have been if
Lord Crawthorne had visited the Cottage when she
was there alone.

What defence would she and Nana have had
against a man like that?

Even now she had the feeling that he would not
give up so easily.

He had wanted to kiss her last night and his desire
had been unmistakable. As she thought of it she remembered his arms pulling her against him.

She could still feel the fierce possessiveness of his
lips against her cheek.

'I hate him! I hate him!' Celesta thought.

She remembered how she had run from the arbour
into the Earl's arms and found a feeling of security
and safety to replace her fear.

He had seemed so big and strong standing there
in the light of the Chinese lantern.

There was nothing Lord Crawthorne could do in
his presence.

But the Earl was in London and Lord Crawthorne
was at this moment in the Sitting-Room with Giles,
whispering poisonous ideas into his mind, inciting him

to further hatred against the man who had rescued
him from prison.

"How can Giles listen to His Lordship?" Celesta
asked.

Then she felt a warm feeling in her heart because
Giles had refused to let Lord Crawthorne talk with
her alone.

She was deep in thought and had not even picked
up the sewing which occupied her leisure hours when
she heard Giles calling to her from the bottom of the
stairs:

"Celesta! Come down!"

Reluctantly Celesta obeyed him and found him
waiting for her.

His face looked flushed and there was a glint of
excitement in his eyes she did not understand.

"His Lordship is going back to London," he said,
"and he wishes to bid you good-bye."

Celesta was so pleased that Lord Crawthorne was
leaving that she entered the Sitting-Room with a smile
on her lips.

"I must thank you, Celesta," he said, "for an excellent luncheon. It has been an inexpressible pleasure
to see you, and when I have gone Giles will tell you
what we have discussed about the future."

"The future?" Celesta asked sharply.

"I shall be seeing you not tomorrow but the next
day," Lord Crawthorne said.

Celesta looked at him uncertainly as he went on:

"I have not had a chance to tell you how beautiful
you looked last night."

Celesta was surprised that he should refer to the
evening when he had been humiliated in front of her,
but she merely inclined her head.

"A great number of people will be talking about
you today," Lord Crawthorne said. "Most of their re-
marks will be complimentary, although some, like
Lady Imogen for instance, will be full of envy, hatred
and malice."

Celesta looked uncomfortable.

She was remembering the anger on Lady Imogen's face when the Earl had led her from the Supper-Room.

"But then, of course," Lord Crawthorne continued, "poor Lady Imogen has every reason to be jealous. It is doubtful if any woman could keep Meltham faithful to her for long!"

Celesta was very still.

There was an innuendo in Lord Crawthorne's voice that was unmistakable and as she did not speak he added:

"Of course you know that they are to be married? The Wedding is arranged to take place early in the Autumn when the King returns to London."

Celesta felt as if Lord Crawthorne had thrust a dagger into her heart.

She did not understand the pain or why the sunshine had gone and the small Sitting-Room seemed dark.

"They . . . they are to be . . . married?" she questioned in a low voice, aware that Lord Crawthorne's eyes were on her face.

"Did not Meltham tell you?" he asked. "That is not surprising! Imogen will have a difficult life with such a rake! Nevertheless from her point of view marriage has its compensations!"

"At least the Earl is rich and can buy her everything her heart desires," Giles interposed with a bitter note in his voice.

"Yes, the Earl is a very rich man," Lord Crawthorne said, "and let us hope for Lady Imogen's sake he lives to enjoy it!"

He took Celesta's hand as he spoke and raised it to his lips.

"You refused my present," he said softly, "but when I come again I will bring you something different—something which I know you will accept!"

Celesta felt his lips on her skin but somehow it made no impact on her.

She did not even shrink from him.

She merely felt numb, as if her whole body had become paralysed.

She was aware that Giles was escorting Lord Crawthorne to his carriage and they were talking intimately with their heads close together as they went down the garden path.

She could see them from the window but still she did not move.

She could only stand staring across the room and feel as if her feet were weighted down to the floor.

So the Earl was to marry Lady Imogen!

She was not surprised at his choice.

Never had she imagined any woman could be so beautiful as Lady Imogen with her red hair and green eyes.

There was something bewitching about her; something which Celesta was certain any man would find irresistible.

She was very feminine and had the sophisticated elegance and self-assurance that the Earl would require in his wife.

He had said that he had no desire to be married, but that had obviously been merely an excuse for asking her to become his mistress—a mistress whom he would have discarded very quickly because he would have found her dull and uninteresting beside someone like Lady Imogen.

Celesta remembered that strange, unaccountable feeling the Earl had aroused in her when he had kissed her.

It was a feeling she had been unable to explain, but because of it she had wanted him to go on kissing her and not to stop.

Then as through the window she saw Lord Crawthorne drive away, as she saw Giles walking back towards the house, she knew like a flash of lightning sweeping through her, like a sudden pillar of fire in the sky, that she loved the Earl.

She had loved him, she thought wildly, from the very first moment when he had kissed her in the peach-house and she had been unable to fight against him.

When he had called on her she had tried to hate him.

Yet when they had dined together and she had come down the Library steps to find him standing at the bottom of them she had no hate in her heart.

She should have known then, she thought, that the strangely unaccountable sensation he aroused in her was love.

She should have known when they stood together in the Priests' hole and she wondered whether he would put his arms round her that she already loved him.

It had been an excitement, a kind of thrilling anticipation that was half fear, half pleasure.

But nothing like the frightening terror that Lord Crawthorne evoked in her.

She was in love and she had not known it!

She loved the Earl and only now, when she had lost him, did she understand why when he had held her in his arms she had known a security and a feeling of safety that was beyond anything she had ever experienced before.

"I love him! I love him!" she told herself and knew with a feeling of abject despair that he was to marry Lady Imogen.

He would no longer trouble himself with her.

What he had said and done last night was merely an act of kindness.

It had perhaps seemed to him pathetic that she had never been to a Ball and that she had suffered, as he had said the first time they talked, from "the sins that she had not herself committed."

"How could I have imagined for one moment that I could mean anything to him when I live in the shadow of sin?" Celesta asked.

An incoherent tempest of thoughts rushed through her mind.

Then she realised that Giles was delaying coming

into the Sitting-Room because he was opening another bottle of brandy, which he had taken from the case in the Hall.

He came into the room having extracted the cork and filled his glass.

Then he raised it to Celesta.

"Congratulate me!" he said. "I have pulled off a tremendous coup—something you never thought I would do!"

"What is it? What has Lord Crawthorne suggested to you?" Celesta asked.

Giles took a long drink of the brandy.

"You can be proud of your brother," he said, "and I can assure you I am very proud of myself! We are in clover, Celesta!"

"What are you talking about, Giles?" Celesta asked. "Tell me because I am worried."

"There is no need to be worried," Giles replied. "We are going to sit pretty and enjoy ourselves, and the person you have to thank is me!"

"What have you done?" Celesta asked with a touch of irritation in her voice.

She did not like the way that Giles was boasting or care for the bombastic note in his voice.

What could Lord Crawthorne possibly have done, she wondered, to evoke such elation?

"I give you three guesses," Giles said. "Three guesses, Celesta, as to what I have pushed Crawthorne into suggesting where you are concerned."

There was a sudden silence.

"Where . . . I am concerned?" Celesta repeated.

"Yes—you!" Giles said. "He had very different intentions when he came here, which was proved by that diamond bracelet you so sensibly refused."

"Intentions?" Celesta echoed. "I can quite believe that his intentions are disgusting and depraved, whatever they may be."

"Oh no! That is where you are quite wrong, my dear sister," Giles said. "His Lordship's intentions, now that I have explained things a little more clearly, are strictly honourable!"

There was a silence while Celesta felt as though her heart would stop beating.

Then in a voice which seemed almost to choke her with the words she said:

"What are you . . . trying to say to . . . me? What do you . . . mean by 'strictly honourable'?"

"I mean, Celesta, that he is willing to marry you!" Giles said. "You can thank me for the best offer you are ever likely to receive!"

"Marry him?" Celesta enquired. "Are you crazy? Do you really believe that I would marry a man like that?"

"Of course you will marry him," Giles said sharply. "I have already given him my word that you will do so."

"You must be out of your mind!" Celesta cried. "I would not marry Lord Crawthorne if he were the last man on earth! Anything you may have said on my behalf you will have to contradict."

Giles moved to stand in front of the fireplace, and his eyes narrowed in a manner Celesta had noticed before.

He looked at her as she faced him defiantly, and for a moment she thought he was going to rage at her.

Instead he said in a voice that was unexpectedly firm:

"As you well know, you have no say in the matter."

"What do you mean?" Celesta asked.

"You are only eighteen," Giles replied, "and I am your Guardian."

There was a silence, then he went on:

"Have you forgotten that a Guardian has complete and absolute power over his Ward?"

Celesta did not speak and he continued:

"Just as Papa could have accepted any young man who wished to pay his addresses to you, so now I am in that position, and let me make it quite clear, Celesta, I have accepted Lord Crawthorne's proposal that you should be his wife!"

"I will not . . . marry him!" Celesta said in a low voice. "I would rather . . . die!"

"You will marry him because he will provide for you in the future," Giles said, "and for me in the present."

"What has he promised you? What bribe has he offered to make you even consider anything as impossible?" Celesta asked wildly.

"He has promised me that I shall go back to London and live the life I enjoy," Giles answered. "He has also assured me—and I believe him—that we can arrange for the Priory to become my property again."

"You have had too much to drink!" Celesta said. "To begin with, Giles, you cannot dispose of me as if I were some inanimate object you could give away without a thought for my feelings."

Giles did not answer and she said quickly:

"Secondly you cannot be so foolish as to imagine there is any possible way that you could regain the Priory from the Earl. He won it gaming, as both you and I know, and a gambling debt is one of honour."

"You are very voluble," Giles said disagreeably. "But why should I listen to you? Crawthorne is going to arrange that your marriage will take place quickly and quietly, because I cannot afford any expense."

"I will not marry him!" Celesta cried. "Will you not get it into your head, Giles, that I will not marry him? I loathe and detest him!"

"Who cares what your feelings in the matter are?" Giles asked. "It will mean that we shall be rich and comfortable and live the life we want to live."

His voice sharpened as he went on:

"If you think I am going to give up what Crawthorne has offered me for the sake of some foolish, girlish simperings on your part, you are very much mistaken!"

Celesta went to his side and put out her hand.

"Please, Giles, do not quarrel," she begged. "Try to

understand my point of view. I detest Lord Craw-thorne!"

"What does it matter?" Giles asked. "I am not pre-tending he will make you a very attractive husband, but he will support you, Celesta, and while he is enamoured of you as he is at the moment, you can do anything you like with him."

"I do not want to do anything with him," Celesta said almost childishly. "Why has he no wife? Why is he not married?"

"He has been married twice, as it happens," Giles answered. "His first wife died and his second took her own life!"

"Because I presume she could not tolerate His Lord-ship any longer," Celesta said. "Do you wish that to happen to me?"

"You are being hysterical!" Giles replied unsympa-thetically. "Crawthorne is all right and he can be a good friend if it suits him, which it does at the mo-ment."

"Only because he wants me!" Celesta said percep-tively. "Do you think he will go on being a good friend when I no longer interest him? When he is bored with me and finds other women more interest-ing?"

"By that time," Giles answered complacently, "I shall have feathered my nest, and I will be back in the Priory!"

"What has Lord Crawthorne said about the Priory?" Celesta asked.

Giles walked to the table to pour himself another drink.

"I am not going to tell you anything," he said. "I do not trust you! But Crawthorne is clever."

"How is he clever about the Priory?" Celesta per-sisted.

"He has told me not to tell you."

Giles sat down in a chair, sipping his brandy.

"If you tell me what I want to know," Celesta

coaxed, "perhaps I will be more . . . pleasant to him when he comes to see me again."

Giles was getting very drunk, but at the same time she realised that what she had said had percolated his mind.

"I might behave very . . . badly if you do not tell me," she threatened.

Giles considered this for a moment and then he said, his voice thick:

"Crawthorne thinks that we can prove that Meltham broke the rules of the game and that his bid for the Priory was not valid because Crawthorne himself had already wagered the same amount."

"If that was true, why did he not say so at the time?" Celesta asked.

"Meltham is rich and money talks, as you well know, Celesta," Giles answered. "But if Meltham was not there, then it might be quite easy to prove."

"What do you mean, 'if he was not there'?" Celesta enquired.

There was a pause. She had the feeling that Giles was thinking up an answer rather than telling her the truth.

"He could be abroad on his honeymoon, for one thing," Giles replied at last.

Even as he spoke Celesta was sure that that was not the answer he should have given.

Chapter Seven

The Earl rose early despite the fact that he had gone to bed very late after his Ball.

As he dressed he decided he would go to Wroxley Priory. He summoned his Secretary and gave him instructions to send a groom ahead to prepare the House-Hold.

"I have a letter here," the Earl continued, "for *Mademoiselle* Désirée Lafette. Will you take it to her personally and hand her over the deeds of the house."

The Secretary looked surprised and said tentatively:

"You will remember, My Lord, we had some difficulty in finding a house to purchase in that particular locality."

"I will not be needing it again," the Earl said briefly.

"Very good, My Lord."

There were various other matters to be seen to and just as the Earl had finished dealing with them, a note arrived from Carlton House asking him to see the King immediately after luncheon.

This upset all the Earl's plans.

"I am afraid I shall have to postpone going to the country until tomorrow," he said to his Secretary.

"There would indeed hardly be time for you to go, My Lord, unless His Majesty requires you for a very short time."

The Earl smiled.

His Majesty's "short times" usually involved a commitment of several hours.

"I have a feeling the King wishes to talk over the Coronation with me," he said.

"I expect that that is the explanation, My Lord," his Secretary agreed.

The Earl therefore repaired to his Club for an early luncheon and found Captain Charles Kepple, as he had expected, in the Morning-Room.

"Good-morning, Vidal," Charles Kepple said. "I have been hearing glowing accounts of your Ball last night."

"I am only sorry you could not be there," the Earl replied.

"It was just my luck to be on guard duty when you were giving a party," Charles Kepple said, "and as you can imagine on Coronation night no-one wished to exchange duties with me."

"I hear there were a number of very noisy junketings all over London," the Earl said as he sat down in a chair next to his friend.

"But your party was exceptional!" Charles Kepple said.

"To what are you referring particularly?" the Earl enquired with a twinkle in his eyes.

Charles Kepple laughed.

"You know as well as I do! The whole town is talking about the new 'Incomparable' that you produced. Who is she, Vidal?"

"I imagine you are speaking of Miss Celesta Wroxley."

"Giles Wroxley's sister? How extraordinary!"

"Why extraordinary?" the Earl asked.

"Since you won her brother's Estate at cards it would seem strange that she should be on nodding acquaintance with you, let alone being the Belle of your Ball!"

The Earl made no comment and his friend, who knew him well, realised he did not wish to talk about it.

At the same time Charles Kepple could not help saying mischievously:

"I hear Lady Imogen's nose is out of joint! A good thing too!"

138 BARBARA CARTLAND

Still the Earl said nothing and Charles Kepple, who was always irrepressible, continued:

"You know she has been telling everyone that you and she are to be married in the Autumn? I am thinking that after what they saw last night, no-one in future is likely to believe her."

The Earl looked startled.

"Had she really gone as far as that?"

"And a good deal further, but I will not bore you with the details."

"No, I do not wish to hear them. Let us go into luncheon."

They talked of racing and other more immediate matters until it was time for the Earl to leave for Carlton House.

The King hurried across the room the moment he was announced.

"I am glad you could come, Meltham. I must have your advice."

"About what, Sire?" the Earl asked in surprise.

He had been quite certain, as he had told his Secretary, that the reason he had been invited to Carlton House was to talk over details of the Coronation.

"About the Queen," the King replied.

"What has happened? What has Her Majesty done?" the Earl asked hastily.

He felt it could not be anything very dramatic or else Charles Kepple and other members of his Club would have heard about it.

"She is ill!" the King answered.

"But Her Majesty was well enough yesterday when she tried to get into the Abbey," the Earl replied.

"I have heard about that," the King answered. "But apparently when she reached home she collapsed and is drugging herself on laudanum and other medicines. I am informed she is really ill."

The Earl was well aware that the King had his spies in the Queen's House-Hold and, if he had been told that Her Majesty was really ill, then it was likely to be the truth.

"There is nothing you can do about it, Sire," he said firmly.

"What is worrying me," the King said, "and why I need your advice, is that I am making arrangements to visit Ireland. If the Queen gets worse and dies, would I have to cancel my visit? It would cause a great deal of commotion! As you can imagine, State Visits are expensive for all concerned."

The Earl thought for a moment.

He was not surprised that the King had consulted him on what was really a political issue.

On a number of occasions as Regent, the King had found his advice far more sensible and unbiased than those of his Statesmen.

"I should go ahead with your preparations, Sire," the Earl said. "After all, no-one will expect you to mourn excessively if the Queen dies."

He himself thought it was unlikely that the Queen's condition was as bad as it was being made out to be.

At the same time, she was such an unpredictable woman that it would be quite in character for her to die at an inconvenient time, just to spite her husband.

"No, you are right. A few days should be sufficient," the King said reflectively. "Besides, I am most anxious to go to Ireland. At the same time . . ."

He paused for a moment, then said in a low voice:

"As you are well aware, Meltham, I dislike having to leave Lady Conyngham."

The Earl was amused.

Everyone knew that the previous year the King had fallen over-whelmingly in love with the fat, kindly, religious, rapacious Lady Conyngham, who was fifty-two.

She had been married for twenty-seven years and had four grown-up children.

Her beauty was beginning to fade and she had never been particularly intelligent.

Yet the King adored her!

What was more, Lady Conyngham was making the very most of his infatuation.

Sir Benjamin Bloomfield, Keeper of the Privy Purse, said quite openly:

"It is quite shameful the way in which Lady Conyngham is covered with jewels. I believe the King has given her a hundred thousand pounds' worth."

This was not surprising as Lady Conyngham was exceptionally fond of jewellery.

One of her proudest possessions was a sapphire surrounded by brilliants which had belonged to the Stuarts and had been given by Cardinal York to the King.

The Pamphleteers and Cartoonists had enjoyed a field-day, drawing and describing the love-affair between two elderly and exceedingly fat people.

All London had laughed only the previous week at a couplet which ran:

> *Quaffing their claret, then mingling their lips,*
> *Or tickling the fat about each other's hips.*

The King, who had always been emotional and theatrical in all his love-affairs, had not changed with the years.

The Princess Leven, wife of the Russian Ambassador, had related that the King had told her he had "never known what it was like to be in love before," and he would do anything on earth for Lady Conyngham, as "she is an angel sent from Heaven for me."

Looking at the worried expression on the King's face, the Earl realised now that he was definitely perturbed at the thought of going to Ireland without Lady Conyngham at his side, and he could not help feeling sorry for him.

No-one knew better than the Earl how lonely the King felt at times.

Despite his innumerable love-affairs, the King would have been happier as a husband and a father.

He had always fallen in love with women older than himself, which showed his sense of insecurity, but he adored having his advice asked by the young.

As if he felt the Earl's sympathy the King said:

"I have something to show you, Meltham."

The Earl fancied he would have to admire a new picture or expensive *Objet d'Art* such as the King purchased almost every day of his life.

But to his surprise when the King led him into an Ante-Room he saw lying on one of the sofas a pile of children's toys.

There were dolls and lead soldiers, boxes of nine-pins, play-horses, miniature farm-yards, and games and toys of every description.

The Earl stared at them in astonishment and the King said:

"These of course are for the Conynghams. I want you to realise, Meltham, how much it means that I can share their family life and how deeply I regret now never having had such a family of my own."

The Earl was silent.

He saw that the King's eyes were misting as they always did when he thought of his only child, the Princess Charlotte, who two years ago had died in child-birth.

Then he went on:

"But I am fortunate, Meltham, very fortunate that Lady Conyngham has come into my life and changed it completely."

The Earl had picked up a doll with fair hair.

"I love her children," the King was saying, "as if they were my own! You will be interested, I know, to see a letter from her younger daughter, Maria, who wrote to me only this morning."

As he spoke the King proudly drew a letter from his pocket.

The Earl put down the doll and read the letter. He saw it was very affectionate.

"I am glad this can bring you such happiness, Sire," he said.

"And you still think I should go to Ireland?"

"Yes, I am convinced Your Majesty should do so,"

the Earl replied. "Your Irish subjects will be over-
whelmingly delighted to see you."

"Then I shall go on with my arrangements," the
King said firmly.

The King then insisted on taking the Earl to inspect
some new pictures which had just arrived from Hol-
land and a sketch that had been made of the Coronation.

By the time the Earl returned home it was definitely
far too late to leave for the country.

He was therefore determined to go to Wroxley
Priory the following morning.

There again however he was circumvented by his
Secretary, who remembered that he had promised to
speak in a Debate that was taking place that afternoon in the House of Lords.

As he had seen the Peer whose Bill he was supporting the previous day when he had lunched at his
Club, the Earl felt it would be unnecessarily rude to
default at the last moment.

He therefore was obliged to repair to the House of
Lords to make an eloquent and erudite speech to
which he was quite certain none of the Peers listened.

It was six o'clock before eventually he could leave
London.

He drove his own phaeton and moving swiftly
through the traffic he thought with satisfaction that he
would reach Wroxley Priory in time for a late dinner.

Celesta had awakened that morning determined
that she would try to persuade Giles that she could
not marry Lord Crawthorne.

She had gone to bed in tears after realising that
having finished a second bottle of brandy her brother
was in no fit state to listen to whatever she might have
to say on the subject.

When she was alone in the darkness of her small
room, she had cried uncontrollably and despairingly,
and had known it was not only because her future was

dominated by Lord Crawthorne, but also because she had lost the Earl.

She admitted to herself now that she had thought almost exclusively of him ever since they had first met.

He had always been there in her thoughts, and in some strange way he was already a part of her life.

When they had danced together at his Ball she had felt it somehow symbolic of how close they were to each other in everything they thought and felt.

She went over and over again in her mind the subjects they had discussed that first night when she had dined with the Earl at the Priory.

She had believed that she hated him not only because he had won her home at cards but also because he had kissed her.

She now knew that the feeling she had for him from the very beginning was because he disturbed her as a man.

He was so vitally masculine, and yet strangely she was not afraid of him as she was of Lord Crawthorne.

Instead he gave her a feeling of safety which she had not known since her mother had run away.

But the Earl was to be married and now he was lost to her for ever.

She could not understand why he had been so kind or indeed so flattering when his heart was already engaged with Lady Imogen.

Then she told herself humbly that it was because she was of no consequence. She was outside the bounds of Society and therefore he could treat her as a light woman, a prospective mistress.

And yet he had asked her to his Ball and introduced her to his friends.

What was more, he deliberately invited their comments by singling her out for his attentions.

Celesta could not understand it at all; yet she felt there must be an explanation.

Whatever it was, she felt as if her brain would not function, could not sort out any problem, however simple, because the pain in her heart could only make her weep.

She cried and cried and awoke in the morning looking very pale with dark lines under her eyes.

"Lawks-a-merry! What have you been doing to yourself, Miss Celesta?" Nana exclaimed as soon as she saw her.

Celesta did not answer and Nana went on:

"I knows as how you don't want to marry His Lordship, dearie. At the same time you couldn't go on living for ever in this Cottage with only me to look after you. You're too beautiful, and that's the truth. It would end in trouble sooner or later!"

"Nothing could be worse trouble than it is at the moment," Celesta said in a low voice. "I hate His Lordship! I would rather handle a snake than endure his kisses!"

Nana sighed but she offered no solution.

Celesta knew that actually Nana was relieved that she had received an offer of marriage.

The slights and snubs she had had to endure after her mother ran away had hurt not only her, they had hurt Nana too.

Now, however repulsive the bride-groom, she would be Lady Crawthorne and entitled to the respect and courtesy of those who had ostracised her in the past.

"Yet I would rather scrub floors or beg in the streets than be married to such a man!" Celesta told herself.

When Giles finally appeared downstairs just before luncheon she knew by the expression in his eyes when he looked at her that she would receive no sympathy from him.

He had everything to gain by her marriage, and while she was certain that Lord Crawthorne would soon grow bored with being generous to his brother-in-law, Giles was content for the moment.

He had the chance to escape from the confines of the tiny Cottage and he craved for London in the same way he craved for drink.

The afternoon passed slowly, but it was a relief to

remember that Lord Crawthorne had said he would not come that day but the day after.

'Giles had said we were to marry quickly,' Celesta thought. 'How quickly and where will it take place?'

She felt sick at the thought of being the wife of a man she loathed and detested, and yet there seemed little she could do.

She knew only too well that when Giles was determined about something it was impossible to make him change his mind.

He was quite capable, if it suited him, of dragging her up the aisle and she knew that he intended to watch her every movement until the ring was actually on her finger.

She felt so tired and listless after the tears she had shed all night that when Nana suggested she should lie down in the afternoon she agreed.

She went up to her room and while she lay on her bed she found herself going over and over in her mind the impossible position in which she found herself.

She knew that had she not known that the Earl was engaged to be married, she would have gone to him and begged him to save her.

But she had seen Lady Imogen's face at the Ball when he told her why he had not taken her down to supper, and Celesta was well aware that she had made an implacable enemy.

Under the circumstances how could she ask the Earl to rescue her? Indeed there was nothing he could do since she was under age and Giles was her Guardian.

She told herself that probably the Earl and Lady Imogen had had a quarrel and that was why he had ignored her at the Ball.

Doubtless after she and Giles had left for the country they had made it up.

She imagined the Earl's lips on Lady Imogen's exquisite curved mouth, and the pain of such a thought was almost unbearable.

Celesta remembered the firm possessiveness of his lips.

It made her feel again that strange, warm, insidious rapture which crept over her until the world slipped away, leaving nothing but the strength of his arms and the pressure of his mouth.

"It was love!" she told herself.

Very slowly the tears gathered in her eyes and ran down her cheeks.

Later she must have slept for a little while because when Nana came in she woke with a start.

Then she knew she had been happy because she had imagined that once again she had been dancing with the Earl.

"It'll soon be dinner-time, dearie," Nana said, "and Master Giles is downstairs alone drinking. You'd best go and talk to him."

"I should not have left him alone," Celesta said, rising from the bed.

She realised as she did so that Nana was hesitating near the door as if she had something to say.

"What is it, Nana?"

"I've just heard," Nana answered, "that they're expecting His Lordship at the Priory this evening."

Celesta felt her heart give a sudden leap. Then she told herself that she had no right to feel that way.

"What time is he arriving, Nana?"

The question was out before she could prevent it.

"I've no idea," Nana answered, "but apparently His Lordship is expected alone."

'I shall see him! I shall see him!'

Celesta felt her heart singing the words.

She felt herself come alive. The dark despair which had made her lethargic all day seemed to slip away from her.

But he was engaged to be married!

A picture of Lady Imogen's lovely face swam in front of Celesta's eyes—the dark-fringed green eyes, the flaming red hair!

How could she bear to think of them together?

Suddenly Celesta knew what she must do.

The idea was so revolutionary she could only stand still, uncertain whether it had come into her mind involuntarily or whether somebody had suggested it to her.

Nana had gone downstairs.

"I will leave tomorrow," Celesta told herself.

Then going to a cupboard in her room she seldom used, she looked inside.

Hanging beside the gown she had worn at the Earl's Ball were the other garments that her mother had sent her from Paris over the last four years.

On the floor in white boxes were presents she had received on her birthday and at Christmas, or sometimes on random occasions.

Celesta looked at them for a long time. Then she shut the door and, creeping along the passage so that neither Giles nor Nana should hear her, she went up the tiny narrow stairs which led to the attic.

Here, neatly piled, were the trunks which had come with them from the Priory.

There was a small leather box with a curved top that was not too heavy. This Celesta carried down, negotiating the stairs with some difficulty, and took it into her bed-room.

She would have to think of some way in which, having packed it, she could get it to the Stage-coach without Giles being aware that she was leaving.

Nana would help her, she was sure of that, even though she might disapprove of what she was going to do.

But whatever happened, Giles must not learn her intentions.

All his plans for her marriage and his own return to London would be destroyed if she went away.

"Mama is the only person who can help me now," Celesta told herself.

She hid the trunk and went downstairs to the Sitting-Room.

The Church clock struck two and Celesta, who had turned and twisted in her bed since ten o'clock, rose to pull back the curtains from the window.

There was a pale moon and she could see the world outside bathed in a silver light.

It was very hot and she had a sudden longing for air.

She turned back into her room and put on a cotton wrapper which Nana had made for her to wear in the summer over her thin lawn night-gowns.

She tied the sash of it round her slim waist and, putting on a pair of slippers, opened the door of her room very carefully.

The house was very quiet.

She expected to hear Giles snoring as she had heard him the night before, but there was no sound from his room and to her surprise she saw his door was open.

'He must be downstairs in the Sitting-Room,' she thought, and guessed he had been too drunk to get to bed.

Very quietly Celesta slipped down the stairs.

The Sitting-Room door was shut and she let herself out through the back entrance.

In the garden there was the scent of stocks and roses.

As she moved towards the shrubbery she heard the rustle of small animals in the under-growth and an owl hooted far away in the distance.

Celesta had the idea that if she could walk about, her problems would not seem as insistent as they had when she was lying in her bed.

Was she doing the right thing in going away?

To stay would mean that Giles would force her to marry Lord Crawthorne and she had known from the very beginning that this was impossible.

She had not been exaggerating when she had told Giles that she would rather die than marry him.

It was the truth.

She walked to the edge of the shrubbery and saw

lying ahead of her the Priory in all its beauty.

The moonlight revealed its Elizabethan roofs and twisted chimney stacks and glittered on the diamond-paned windows.

It was very beautiful. Celesta had always felt even as a child that it still had a spiritual, almost holy atmosphere about it, as if the influence created by the monks had never been erased by time.

It had been her home and now it belonged to the man she loved.

She wondered how soon the Earl would bring Lady Imogen there and remembered how she had said what a perfect place it would be for a fancy-dress Ball.

"I might go as the family ghost!" Lady Imogen had laughed. "I am sure there is one!"

Celesta had the uncanny feeling that she was in fact a ghost haunting the Priory.

Perhaps because she was there in spirit the Earl would sometimes remember her.

It was so painful to think of him and know that he was sleeping in the Master Bed-Room that Celesta turned from looking at the house and moved away.

She walked along a mossy path to where the shrubbery joined the pine-wood which encircled the back of the house, protecting it from the North-East winds that at times blew fiercely from the sea.

Her footsteps made no sound as she moved through the trees, drawing nearer to the house, while at the same time it was out of her sight.

Then as she walked along, deep in her thoughts, suddenly she heard someone speaking.

She stopped still, realised that it was a man's voice and he was somewhere just ahead of her.

She wondered who it could be.

When her father was alive she would have expected it would be a Game-Keeper either hunting vermin or watching for poachers.

But the Game-Keepers had all been dismissed, and

she knew that if the Earl had engaged new ones it
would have been talked about in the village.

"Why then," she asked herself, "should there be men
in the woods at this time of night?"

Curious and hidden by the branches of the trees,
she moved on.

Peeping through the thick leaves of a rhododendron
bush, she saw two men sitting on the ground at the
foot of a tall fir-tree.

There was a small clearing and the ground was
sandy beneath the firs.

Celesta knew beyond it there was a path which
led from there directly to the back of the Priory.

"Wot's th'time?" one of the men was asking.

Now she could see that they were rough and uncouth men with handkerchiefs round their necks and
felt hats pulled low over their eyes.

The man who had spoken had a cockney accent.

In answer his companion pulled a watch from his
pocket.

"'Tis nigh on twenty past," he answered. "Us goes
in 'nother two minutes as 'is Nibs told we."

"What'll us do if anyun sees we?" the first man
asked and there was a nervous note in his voice.

"'Ow can us be seen if us goes up the secret passage?" the older man replied. "'E's told Oi exactly
where it is and once we're inside we're safe."

"I 'opes ye're right!"

"Now all ye 'as to do, Sam, is wot ye're been told.
Ye goes first—stabs 'im if 'e be asleep an' only if 'e
fights ye, do Oi shoot 'im."

"Oi knows! Oi knows!" the younger man said, "and
then us nips back down the passage an' back 'ere."

"Where 'is Nibs'll be awaiting with th' money—make
no mistake abaht that Gold, Sam! And that's what us
both wants."

As he spoke the older man got to his feet.

"Cum on now! An' whatever 'appens, don't panic!"

"'Tis all right for ye to say that," Sam whined,

"but Oi've got to stab 'im, an' wot'll Oi do if 'e ain't asleep?"

"Cum on!" was the answer, and the two men moved through the trees towards the house.

Celesta stood as if turned to stone.

Now she understood!

Now she knew what Giles had meant when he had said:

"It would be easier to prove the Earl had broken the rules of the game if he was not there."

Then she remembered something else; remembered Lord Crawthorne saying in that slimy, silky voice:

"The Earl is a very rich man and let us hope for Lady Imogen's sake he lives to enjoy it!"

She knew what was being planned.

She knew why Giles and Lord Crawthorne had whispered together in the Sitting-Room and her brother had been so sure that he would be able to get the Priory back into his possession.

Giles would be a murderer!

She could hardly credit the truth that he had instigated the crime that was about to be committed.

No-one else except for herself and the Earl knew of the secret passage which led directly into the Master Bed-Room.

The thought of the men she had just seen creeping up to the Earl to stab him while he slept galvanised Celesta into action.

She turned and ran back a little way down the path by which she had come. Then when she was opposite the front of the house she sped through the garden towards the Priory.

She crossed the herb-garden and ran on through the roses and down the long grass walk where her mother had planted herbaceous borders.

She was almost breathless with the speed at which she had run by the time she came to the garden door which had been her usual exit from the house when she had lived at the Priory.

The door would be locked. His Lordship's servants

would have seen to that. But the catch on the casement window on one side of it had been broken for
years and no-one had ever bothered to have it repaired.

Celesta pulled at the lead window-frame and, as she
expected, it opened quite easily.

It took her only a second to slip over the window-
sill and into the house.

Then because it was all so familiar to her she ran,
almost as quickly as she had run through the garden,
along the passages and up the twisting old stairway
which led to the first floor.

The Master Bed-Room was still some distance from
the landing which opened on to the main staircase,
and Celesta was frightened that the men might move
quicker than she could, and anyway they had less
distance to go.

The house was very quiet save for the tick of a
grandfather clock in the Hall, and if there was a night-
watchman there was no sign of him.

She reached the door of the Master-Suite and without knocking opened it.

The room was not in darkness because the Earl
on going to bed had pulled back the curtains from
one of the windows.

The casement was wide open and the moonlight
cast a pool of silver light on the worn red carpet.

The big oak four-poster bed was in shadow and as
Celesta moved towards it she could see the Earl's dark
head on the pillow and knew he was asleep.

She realised then how vulnerable he was; how easy
it would be for her if she had a dagger in her hand,
while he was unconscious.

She bent over him and put her hand on his shoulder.

"My Lord!" she whispered.

He woke instantly, like a man who has served in
the Army and is used to being on the alert.

"What is it?" he began.

Then he exclaimed incredulously:

"Celesta! Why are you here?"

"There are two men," she answered quickly. "They are coming up the secret passage to kill you!"

The Earl sat up abruptly.

"What are you talking about?"

He kept his voice low, as if the urgency in hers had made him aware that she was not speaking lightly.

"The first man carries a dagger, the second a pistol!" she said. "But only if you cannot be stabbed to death will they use the pistol."

The Earl got out of bed and reached for his robe, which lay on a chair.

He put it on over his night-shirt. Being dark in colour it made him less conspicuous.

"Have you a pistol?" Celesta whispered.

"No. I can manage without one."

He looked round the room as if, she thought, for a weapon but instead he took her by the hand to a chest of drawers that was set across one corner.

"Get behind it," he said. "Crouch down and do not show yourself."

She obeyed him without argument.

Then raising her eyes just above the top of the chest she watched him move swiftly across the room towards the fireplace.

The panel into the Priests' hole at the top of the secret passage was on the right of the hearth and she wondered what the Earl was about to do.

He bent down and picked up a heavy iron poker which lay in the grate.

He flattened himself against the wall just by the entrance to the secret passage.

For a moment there was absolute silence and then Celesta heard the very faint click of the catch which opened the door in the panelling.

It moved open so smoothly that had the Earl been asleep, as he had been when she entered the room, it would not have disturbed him.

Now the head of the first man appeared and he stepped into the room.

He moved so silently that Celesta watching him was certain that he must be an experienced robber and perhaps murderer.

Now as he moved slowly across the floor towards the bed the other man appeared behind him.

The Earl waited until they were both clear of the door and then he struck.

He brought the iron poker down with all his strengh on the head of the man carrying the pistol and he dropped like a log to the floor.

Sam turned round and Celesta gave a little scream as she saw the dagger glitter in the moonlight.

He had no chance to use it for the Earl gave him an upper-cut on the chin which lifted him off the ground to fall with a crash, striking his head against the oak bed-post before he touched the floor.

"That disposes of them!" the Earl said in his normal voice.

As he spoke he bent down to take the pistol from the hand of the man lying completely unconscious from the blow to his head and the dagger from the side of Sam.

Celesta rose behind the chest of drawers and now as he stood in the moonlight, she could see that the Earl was smiling.

He put out his hand.

"Come!" he said. "I must get you away from here before I raise the alarm."

She moved towards him and he put his arm round her as if to protect her from the men lying on the floor.

She was trembling and he said gently:

"It is all right! There is nothing to fear and you have saved my life."

She could not answer because now that the danger was over she was no longer afraid but was trembling because he was close to her, and his arm was round her shoulders.

Still holding her closely, the Earl shut the door of the secret passage and opened the one onto the landing.

"No-one saw you come here?" he asked.

"N-no," she answered and found it hard to recognise her own voice, it was so unsteady.

"How did you know they were coming to kill me?"

"I heard them talking in the woods."

"Why were you in the woods?"

"I could not sleep."

"That was fortunate for me!" he said.

He led her along the landing and when they reached the door of the main staircase he asked:

"Did you come up this way?"

"No," she answered, "I came in by the garden door. There is a catch broken on one of the windows."

"Then you had better leave the same way," he said, "then I will wake my House-Hold."

They went downstairs side by side.

When they reached the garden door the Earl saw the open window. He threw back the bolts and turned the key in the lock.

Then he looked at Celesta.

She was very lovely and ethereal with her fair hair falling over her shoulders.

"Do I really have to say 'thank you' to you for saving my life?"

She looked up at him thinking that with his hair a little tousled and without his high cravat he looked younger and less awe-inspiring.

"What have you done to yourself?" he asked suddenly.

She realised that he must be able to see in the moonlight the dark shadows under her eyes.

"I . . . cannot tell you . . . now," she answered.

"You can tell me later today," he told her. "There is nothing to worry about and we have plans to make."

His voice seemed to die away and then as if he could not help himself he drew her close.

Her face was upturned to his and now, as if neither
of them could prevent it, their lips met.

It was a kiss as smooth and gentle as the moonlight
touching the water.

Then as Celesta's lips clung to his she felt a flame
arise within her and knew that the Earl felt the same.

His lips became insistent, demanding, passionate,
and Celesta felt the rapture of his closeness sweep
away all thought of everything except that once again
she must surrender herself to the wonder of her love.

"I love you!" she wanted to say but it was impossible
to speak.

Then almost before she realised what was happening he had put her outside the door.

"Go home, my darling," he said. "I cannot have
you involved in this mess."

The door shut and Celesta heard him slip the bolts
home.

For a moment she could not move but only feel
something very precious and wonderful had happened
to her.

Then she started to run back the way she had
come, past the herbaceous border, the roses, the herb-
garden, until she was once again in the wood, in the
shadow of the trees.

She reached the path on which she had walked
until she had heard the men talking.

Just for a moment she hesitated and then she knew,
even though she was sure it was Giles who had given
the men their instructions, that she must make certain.

Could he really be waiting for them as they had
said, to give them their money?

Blood money!

Money stained with the blood of the man they were
to murder as he slept!

Because the Earl had escaped death she felt suddenly strong and no longer afraid.

She would confront Giles.

She would tell him what she thought of his despica-
ble action and she would tell him too that after what

he had tried to do she was free of him and she would never, whatever he might say to her, marry Lord Crawthorne.

She reached the clearing where the men had been sitting when she had listened to their conversation. For a moment she thought it was empty.

Then lying on the sand she saw a figure—the figure of a man.

For a moment she could hardly comprehend that it was not some trick of her imagination.

Then she knew that it was Giles who lay there. She was certain even before she reached his side that he was dead!

Chapter Eight

Celesta dropped down on her knees beside her brother and saw in the moonlight the blood seeping through his coat in a dark crimson stain.

He had been shot and she knew even before she touched his forehead that her first intuition had been correct and he was dead!

The way he lay sprawled on the sandy ground told her that he must have fallen as the bullet hit him.

Then in the moonlight she saw that his hand was out-stretched and his first finger was pointing towards some figures in the sand.

She stared at them incredulously.

Written clearly so that there was no mistaking the words she read:

MELTHAM KILLED ME

The last E trailed away as if it had been an effort on the part of the dying man, but the MELTHAM was written clearly and strongly.

Kneeling beside Giles, Celesta stared at the words.

Then she realised, as if someone told her in so many words, what had occurred, who was responsible not only for the writing in the sand but for Giles's death.

One thing was quite obvious. It would have been impossible for the Earl, whom she had found asleep in the Priory, to have murdered anyone and returned to his bed before the assailants reached him through the secret passage.

Giles had therefore been killed while he waited for the men to return to receive gold for the crime he had instigated.

Only Lord Crawthorne would benefit by Giles's death and only Lord Crawthorne would, by the Earl's death, be revenged for the manner in which he had insulted him.

The whole plot seemed to unfold itself before Celesta.

Then bending forward she rubbed out with her hand the incriminating words written in the sand.

There was nothing she could do for Giles except to murmur a prayer that he would rest in peace.

She rose to her feet and looked round the small clearing to see if there was anything else that might be used as incriminating evidence against the Earl.

Then she turned to walk back along the path through the wood which led to the Cottage.

She had felt quite calm when she had knelt beside Giles's body and realised his death was part of a plan to damage the Earl. But when she reached her own bed-room and closed the door behind her she found herself trembling violently.

It seemed hardly credible that since she had left her bed and gone for a walk in the moonlight she had been involved in so many terrible events.

It had been terrifying to over-hear the men planning the murder of the Earl and a humiliation beyond words to know that only one person could have told them of the secret passage by which they could enter his bed-room while he slept.

As if that were not enough she had to face the fact that her brother was dead—killed by the man who had been his evil genius.

Lord Crawthorne had utilised Giles to implicate the Earl in a crime from which he would be unable to defend himself because he too would be dead.

It was clever, Celesta had to admit, but at the same time diabolical!

She could understand now why she had loathed Lord Crawthorne from the very first moment she had come into contact with him, and why she had known instinctively that he was evil and wicked.

He would have achieved two murders if she had
not been able to warn the Earl in time.

Even now it was difficult to realise that she had
saved the man she loved but by a hair's breadth.

Had the assailants been able to enter the Earl's bed-
room while he slept, he would have had no chance of
survival.

Celesta thought of him lying stabbed to death—
dead as Giles was dead—and knew that without him
there would be nothing left for her in life.

As if her legs could no longer support her she sat
down on the bed and faced the fact that she loved
the Earl with her whole being; loved him so much
that everything seemed changed because of her love.

It seemed impossible now to think that once she
had told him that she would never fall in love or that
she believed that the emotion he first aroused in her
was hatred.

Now, even to think of him was to know that since
he had come into her life everything was altered and
that her only hope of Heaven was to be close to him.

But this she knew was something that must be
denied her, and because she loved him beyond
thought of self, the only thing she could do was to go
away.

When he had kissed her as she left the Priory she
had known that the touch of his lips made them one
person.

She belonged to him and although she knew it was
impossible she had felt just for one moment that he
belonged to her.

They were one! They were indivisible! And then
he had released her.

"Go home, my darling," he had said. "I cannot have
you involved in this mess."

But she was involved.

Involved to the point where her own brother had
attempted murder and had in his turn been murdered
by the man to whom she was promised in marriage.

Celesta put her hands over her eyes and tried to think.

But for the moment she felt as if her brain would no longer function and she could only feel weak and helpless with no idea of where she could seek safety.

She wanted to be with the Earl.

She wanted it so desperately that her whole body cried out with an almost physical agony for him. But he was to be married, and if, as she suspected, he was ready to protect her, she was well aware of the damage it could do to him socially.

Lord Crawthorne would never allow him to snatch her away without causing so much trouble that the Earl would suffer because of it.

Celesta could imagine the lengths to which he would go: there was nothing that he would not say or do to defame and besmirch the man he loathed to the point where he would murder him.

"No," Celesta told herself. "I must not inflict myself upon the Earl under those circumstances."

She was sure that he would endeavour to help her but in doing so he must inevitably hurt himself and that she could not allow.

Once again it seemed to her that the shadow of sin which had covered her from the moment her mother had run away not only separated her from any chance of happiness but had even lengthened through Giles's death.

Dead or alive he was still a man who had tried to commit murder.

That he had failed in his attempt had merely been through the outside chance of her over-hearing his accomplices in the wood.

Celesta could feel again the breathless fear which had made her run across the garden, climb into the Priory, and speed up the stairs to the Earl's bed-room.

Supposing she had been too late?

She could hardly bear to think of it.

She had saved him, but now she must do more. She must go out of his life.

He was to marry Lady Imogen and while perhaps
sometimes he might remember the strange and wonderful magic of their kiss, it would not deflect him
from his social obligations or the fact that he could
offer her nothing but what he called his "protection."

She remembered how she had said to him:

"I would rather die than accept such a position!"

How ignorant and foolish she had been!

Celesta knew now that she could imagine nothing
more wonderful than to know that the Earl would
protect her against all fears and horrors that still
existed round her.

Giles was dead but Lord Crawthorne was alive, and
though there was no legal means by which he could
compel her to marry him she had the feeling that
while His Lordship still desired her he would never
let her go.

"I must get away!" she told herself.

She rose to her feet. Suddenly galvanised into action
by a fear which gave her an unprecedented energy,
she packed the trunk she had brought to her bed-room
earlier in the evening.

All the clothes her mother had sent to her, which
she had not even looked at after their arrival, she took
from the cupboard and placed in the trunk.

There were more than she had thought to find, because hating the gifts she had not counted them or
thought of them again after Nana told her what the
boxes contained.

The stars had faded and the moon vanished from
the sky when finally the cupboard was empty and the
trunk was full.

It was then at last that Celesta lay down on her
bed to close her eyes.

She was well aware that she would need all her
strength not only for the journey ahead but also to
convince Nana that she must go.

She rested but she could not sleep.

At seven o'clock she was up and dressing herself in

an elegant gown of pale blue silk with a coat to cover it of a darker tone.

It was smart! It was Parisian! It was chic!

There was a bonnet to accompany it, high-crowned, trimmed with twisted blue ribbons which tied under her chin, the brim edged with a tiny row of lace which softly framed her little face.

But Celesta hardly looked at herself in the glass.

She had only just finished dressing when the door opened and Nana came in to call her.

For a moment she stood transfixed in the doorway and then as Celesta turned round to face her gave a little cry.

"You're going away, dearie?"

"I am going to Mama."

Nana did not speak and Celesta went on hastily:

"I have to go, Nana, and please, I beg of you, to lend me the money Giles repaid you two days ago. You know that I will pay it back. I cannot stay here, and only Mama will understand that I cannot marry Lord Crawthorne."

Celesta had decided not to tell Nana that Giles was dead. She would learn it soon enough.

Besides, if she did so, there must be explanations as to why she was in the wood and why having found him she had sent no-one to carry his body back to the Cottage.

She saw by the expression in Nana's face that she was about to argue at her assertion that she would not marry Lord Crawthorne and she said quickly:

"There is no haste in such matters. Whatever I do later, at this moment I must see Mama."

"You're right, dearie," Nana said reluctantly. "Perhaps I should have sent you there sooner but you had such a hatred for Her Ladyship and would never speak of her."

Celesta drew a deep breath.

How could she explain to Nana that she had not understood?

When she had said to the Earl: "I will never allow

myself to be inveigled into behaving as Mama behaved," she had not known the power of love.

Unawakened and ignorant, how could she have
guessed that he was right when he had replied, "Love
is a rapture—an over-whelming force which is irresistible"?

Every word made her want to tell him it was the
truth.

Her love for him was indeed a rapture and a wonder since the first moment he had kissed her. It was
also an over-whelming force that she could not resist.

"I love him! I love him!" Celesta wanted to cry out.

But she knew that Nana must not learn of her feelings; otherwise it would seem even more incomprehensible that she must go away to her mother in
Paris.

Saying very little, which afterwards Celesta thought
surprising, Nana brought her savings and put them
into her hands.

"When I get to Paris," Celesta said in a low voice,
"I will write to you, but do not tell anyone where I
have gone."

"What shall I say to His Lordship?"

"If you are speaking of Lord Crawthorne," Celesta
replied, "tell him I have gone North to visit relatives.
Promise me, Nana, you will convince him that he cannot get in touch with me."

"I'll try, dearie," Nana replied.

The first Dover coach passed through the village at
eight-thirty in the morning.

It had rattled its way from old London Bridge down
the Old Kent Road, through New Cross and Black-
heath to Shooter's Hill, where at The Bull the horses
had been changed for the first time.

Then the coach had continued to Gad's Hill, past
the corpses of highwaymen rotting on the gibbets, to
Wroxbury.

It was a slow cumbersome vehicle which unlike
the faster express coaches stopped at every village.

But Celesta was too anxious to get away from the Cottage to be prepared to wait. She knew that at any moment Giles's body might be found in the wood and be carried home.

Then it would be difficult to explain why she was leaving, and to be seen dressed in blue would cause a great deal of local comment.

It was not until her trunk, which was carried to the coach by one of the village boys, was stowed on the roof along with a motley collection of baggage, some hens in a coop, and several crates of vegetables that Celesta felt she was safe.

Slowly the horses drew away from the village and out into the open country on the way to Rochester and the Medway Flats to Canterbury.

The other occupants of the coach, having stared at Celesta with undisguised curiosity, settled themselves to sleep, read, or eat until they reached the next halt.

After dozens of stops, five changes of horses, and a delay when the Coachman became involved in a wordy controversy on a narrow stretch of road with the driver of a dray as to who should pass first, they did not reach Dover until the afternoon.

Celesta was not unduly worried.

She knew there was a boat which left the harbour at about five o'clock and had resigned herself from the very start to being unable to catch an earlier one.

During the long journey she found herself wondering amongst other things what her mother would think when she appeared.

She felt, however, that the presents which had come year after year, even when she had never acknowledged them, were proof that her mother was still concerned with her well-being.

'How foolish I have been,' Celesta thought, 'to have hated Mama all these years.'

Now because she was in love herself she could understand what her mother had felt for the Marquis of Heron.

It was easy to understand that as a child she had

been deeply shocked by her mother's behaviour and
even now she would not pretend it was anything but
wrong.

And yet there were extenuating circumstances.

While Celesta would not condone the fact that her
mother had run away, she could at least not wholly
condemn her, because now she could understand how
it had happened.

But it was impossible to think for long of anyone
except the Earl.

Always in front of her eyes she could see his handsome face, the cynical smile on his lips, the look in his
eyes which seemed so often to be mocking her.

He was over-whelming and over-powering in many
ways, and yet when they had danced together they
had moved in unison and their steps had matched so
that she was sure that they both thought and felt the
same.

Last night it had seemed to her there had been
something new in his kiss that had not been there
before.

She had moved into his arms because it had been
inevitable; because she told herself now that nothing
could have prevented her at that moment from turning to him and seeking his lips as he had sought hers.

Then at the touch of his mouth she had felt a flame
rise within her.

It was nothing she could explain; nothing she could
really put into words; and yet it seemed as if her
whole being pulsated with new life.

Something that was beautiful and unbelievably com-
pelling!

It was as if he swept her into the star-strewn Heavens and they were one with the Divine!

But almost before she could realise what was happening he had led her outside the Priory and she
heard him lock the door.

"That was the moment," Celesta told herself miser-
ably, "when I left his life for ever!"

It was a pain as if she had a dagger in her heart

to know that she would never see him again, but when she had found Giles dead in the wood, there had been no hope for her love.

Celesta shut her eyes.

She did not hear the other passengers chattering or a man snoring beside her, having drunk heavily at the last halting-place.

She did not hear the thump of the luggage moving about over-head, the Coachman swearing at the horses, or the whirl of the wheels.

All she could hear was the Earl's voice saying: "My darling . . ." in a deep voice which seemed to vibrate through her whole body.

"My darling . . . my darling . . ."

That is what she had been to him at that moment. But never again. It was over! It was finished.

The love which had come into her life was a burning light which had swept away her prejudice, her ignorance, her stupidity.

Only to be . . . extinguished.

Now there was nothing left but the darkness which had been hers for four years.

The shadow of sin!

Not just her mother's but now also Giles's.

As the coach drew up outside The King's Head for the passengers to get out, before proceeding to the ship waiting to carry them across the Channel, Celesta realised that there was a strong wind blowing from the sea.

She had felt it when they had descended from the coach at the last halt and her elegant French bonnet had almost been swept from her head.

The other women travellers had clutched at their skirts, holding them down over their ankles as they hurried into the Posting-House.

Now Celesta could see the waves breaking over the promenade, white-crested as they threw their spray against the grey shingle.

The flag flying from the flag-pole outside The King's

Head was almost being torn into fragments, and as they entered the Inn the Landlord said:

"Ye'll not be leaving tonight, Sirs. No skipper'll set sail in this weather."

"Shall we have to stay here?" Celesta asked in consternation.

"Ye will indeed, Ma'am," the Inn-keeper replied, "unless ye have friends in th' neighbourhood."

"No, I have none," Celesta answered, "and I would be grateful if you could provide me with a bed-room."

"I can do that," the Inn-keeper replied.

He glanced at Celesta's elegant appearance and added:

"And one o' the best, Ma'am!"

Celesta had no time to say more because the other passengers in their turn engaged the Inn-keeper's attention.

She allowed a maid in a mob-cap to escort her upstairs where she was shown into a pleasant low-ceilinged room over-looking the sea.

It was only when her luggage had been brought up by a porter and she had given him a few pence for his pains that she wondered whether she would have enough money for the sea-voyage and the coach she must find in France to convey her to Paris.

She had not anticipated having to stay the night in Dover and was well aware that the few sovereigns that Nana had been able to lend her would not permit any extravagance or indeed any untoward delays on the journey.

The fare for the Channel crossing was half a guinea for a Lady or Gentleman and five shillings for their servant if they had one.

Celesta knew that on reaching France she must ignore the expensive, quicker, and more comfortable *post-chaises*.

They charged one shilling eleven pence a day a post and there were thirty and a half posts between Calais and Paris.

But the much cheaper *Carrosses* and *Coches* meant

that the 183 miles to Paris would entail seven lunches and seven suppers on the road.

This would mean the journey could cost as much as two pounds ten shillings.

"I must eat as little as possible," Celesta said to herself. "At least I can economise on food!"

She took off her blue coat, laid it on the bed, and untied the ribbons of her bonnet.

She was too worried about her finances to stay long in front of the mirror, but she noted that her fair hair released from the confines of the bonnet seemed to spring into place and that her eyes were very dark and anxious in her pale face.

At the same time Celesta thought it was strange that her deep unhappiness and her feeling of despair did not show itself more obviously.

'I must find out the cost of this bed-room,' she thought. 'If it is expensive I must move into a cheaper room.'

Turning from the mirror, she went down the stairs.

The Inn-keeper was waiting at the bottom.

"I wanted to ask you . . ." Celesta began in her soft musical voice, only to be interrupted as the man said:

"I were a-just comin' t'find ye, Ma'am. 'Tis awful crowded in the main Saloon and I thinks ye'd be more comfortable in th'private parlour."

"I wanted to ask you . . ." Celesta began again, only to find that the Inn-keeper was stumping ahead of her down the panelled passage to fling open a door at the end of it.

'Perhaps it will be easier to talk to him somewhere quieter,' Celesta thought.

The noise of voices and laughter from the Saloon and the Public Bar echoed round the passages and made it difficult for her to make herself heard.

She walked through the door the Inn-keeper had opened, intending to turn and ask him to talk to her.

Then before she could speak, almost before she could realise what was happening, she saw that the parlour was not empty.

There was a man standing by the mantelpiece!

She looked at him and felt it was impossible to move.

She heard the door close behind her.

Animated by fear, she would have turned to escape but Lord Crawthorne spoke:

"I have been waiting for you, Celesta."

"Why are . . . you here?"

It seemed to Celesta that her voice sounded weak and as if her lips could not form the words.

He was looking more sinister than ever in dark travelling clothes and polished boots.

"It was not difficult to find out where you had gone," he answered. "Your old Nurse lied quite convincingly, but everyone in the village was ready to tell me that you had left on the Dover coach. I passed you on the road an hour ago."

With an effort and because Celesta would not let him see how afraid she was, she put up her chin.

"I am . . . going to my . . . mother."

"I guessed that was your intention," he replied, "and I shall be delighted to take you to Paris, if that is your wish."

"I have no desire to go anywhere with you, My Lord, nor do I intend to . . . marry you."

He smiled and she thought it made him look more evil and more debauched than before.

"I agree with you that marriage is quite unnecessary," he answered. "We can fare very well together, my pretty one, without involving ourselves in the tortuous legalities of our union."

Celesta looked at him scornfully. It was what she might have expected.

"If you are following in your mother's footsteps," he continued jeeringly, "you can, I assure you, my dear, start your career no more advantageously than with me!"

Celesta felt her temper rising, so she was no longer so afraid.

"How dare you speak to me in such a manner!" she

stormed. "Let me assure you that I have no intention of going anywhere with you, My Lord, nor having anything to do with you. I will sit with the other passengers in the Saloon."

She put her hand out towards the door.

"That would be a mistake," Lord Crawthorne said silkily, "for I assure you I shall follow you. The fact that we were brawling with each other would doubtless cause a great deal of curiosity and speculation."

"Leave me . . . alone!"

"That is something I have no intention of doing! You have promised yourself to me and you must keep your promise."

"I have done nothing of the sort!" Celesta replied. "Giles told you that I must marry you but . . . Giles . . ."

She stopped, realising that what she had been about to say would reveal that she knew of Giles's death.

"But Giles is not with us," Lord Crawthorne interposed, "and therefore we can plan our future for ourselves. Yours and mine, Celesta, for I am determined, and make no mistake about this, for I am a very determined man, that we will be together!"

He moved towards her and there was an expression in his eyes which told Celesta what he was about to do.

She turned to pull open the door but was too late!

With a swiftness she had not expected, his arms went round her and he crushed her against him and pulled her back towards the fireplace.

"You are very desirable!" he said in a thick voice, "and I intend to possess you!"

She struggled against him, but his arms enveloped her so that she could not move and he was very strong.

"Let me . . . go!" she cried desperately and knew that in some horrible manner her resistance excited him.

"You are lovely! Very lovely!" he said, "and when I

have taught you to be a little more womanly, you will be lovelier still!"

There was a passionate desire in the thickness of his voice which made Celesta turn her head away from him, thinking he was seeking her lips.

But instead he toppled her backwards onto the couch which stood beside the hearth.

She screamed, but the weight of his body as he lay on top of her made it hard to breathe.

Smiling at her discomfiture, he took her chin with the fingers of his free hand and forced her face round to his.

She gave a despairing cry as his lips, hard and lustful, were on hers.

She tried in vain to struggle and she felt a degradation and horror that was beyond expression.

It was as if he dragged her down into some foul slime from which she could never escape.

Then as she felt his hand fumbling at her breast there was the sound of the door being flung violently open.

Involuntarily Lord Crawthorne raised his head.

It was the Earl who stood there, seeming too big for the small room.

He looked to Celesta like an avenging angel with his face contorted with anger as he saw what was happening.

He slammed the door to behind him.

He was carrying his tall hat in his hand and, flinging it on the floor, he walked across the room.

Lord Crawthorne attempted to rise but he was too late.

The Earl hit him full on the chin with all the force of his clenched fist and Lord Crawthorne fell to the floor beside the couch.

"How dare you hit me, Meltham!" he cried. "If you want satisfaction we can fight like Gentlemen!"

"Get up, you swine!" the Earl retorted. "I intend to teach you a lesson and I do not fight with murderers!"

"What the devil do you mean by calling me a murderer?" Lord Crawthorne asked.

But as he rose to his feet there was a wary look in his eyes which told Celesta he was uneasy.

She pulled herself to a sitting position on the settee.

Lord Crawthorne attempted to strike the Earl but he was obviously too slow and with two hard professional punches the Earl knocked him down again.

This time His Lordship made no effort to rise.

There was blood oozing from between his lips, but there was still an expression of fanatical hatred in his eyes as he looked up at the Earl towering above him.

"I would like to thrash you insensible," the Earl said and there was no mistaking the raw anger in his voice. "But Miss Wroxley is here and I do not wish her to be in the company of filthy lechers of your type."

"You will—pay for this!" Lord Crawthorne said through gritted teeth.

"I doubt it," the Earl replied, "because in future our paths will not cross."

He paused to add slowly:

"There is a warrant out for your arrest, Crawthorne, for the murder last night of Sir Giles Wroxley in the woods outside the Priory!"

"I do not believe it!" Lord Crawthorne snarled, "and if Giles is dead you cannot prove that I killed him!"

"I can not only prove it," the Earl answered, "but the information is already before the Magistrates."

"It is not possible!" Lord Crawthorne mumbled.

There was no mistaking the pallor on his face which proclaimed his fear.

"There is irrefutable evidence of your crime," the Earl answered, "because after your behaviour at my Ball I suspected you might attempt to abduct or in some way interfere with Miss Wroxley. I therefore arranged for a Bow Street Runner to watch you."

Lord Crawthorne did not move or speak but it was obvious that he was listening.

"The Runner heard you quarrel with Giles last night," the Earl went on. "He was black-mailing you for cheating at cards into marriage with his sister. Your quarrel became violent and in an apparently ungovernable rage you shot him in the back."

Lord Crawthorne stared but he did not speak.

"You then tried to implicate me in your cowardly act," the Earl continued. "The Runner watched you writing my name in the sand."

Lord Crawthorne's tongue wetted his dry lips but still he was silent.

"It was a clever idea," the Earl said mockingly, "but it failed ignominiously. When the Military arrive they will take you to Newgate Prison."

The Earl paused to step back from the fallen man.

"But because," he said sharply, "I have no desire for Miss Wroxley's name to be involved in this unpleasant situation, I am giving you a chance."

"What sort of a—chance?" Lord Crawthorne murmured almost beneath his breath.

"If you can leave the country before the Warrant is executed you will remain a free man," the Earl replied, "but if you are brought to Trial there is no doubt at all that you will be hanged."

The Earl walked across the room and opened the door.

"Get out!" he said harshly, "and do not let me set eyes on you again or I promise you, Crawthorne, nothing will stop me from handing you over to the hangman!"

Lord Crawthorne rose to his feet.

He was beaten and he knew it.

He went from the room without raising his head.

The Earl shut the door behind him and stood looking at Celesta.

She had risen to her feet and now as their eyes met she moved towards him as if she were a ship coming into harbour.

He put his arms about her and held her very close.

She hid her face against his shoulder.

"It is all over, my darling."

She was trembling and he said quietly:

"Where do you want to spend your honeymoon?"

"With . . . you!" she whispered without thinking.

The Earl gave a little laugh.

"That is something of which you can be quite sure," he answered. "I am only sorry that I took so long in reaching you, but I stopped at Canterbury for a Special Licence."

Celesta raised her head.

"You . . . you are to . . . marry . . . Lady Imogen."

"I am to marry no-one but you."

She looked at him for a moment, then deliberately disengaged herself from his arms to walk towards the mantelpiece and stand looking down into the fire.

"No!" she said. "I am going away! You must not be . . . involved with me . . . I should . . . only damage your . . . reputation."

The Earl's expression was very tender but he did not move.

"Do you really believe that?" he asked.

She turned her face towards him, her eyes very dark and troubled.

"It is not only . . . Mama . . . it is . . . Giles. He tried to . . . murder you!"

"But he did not succeed—thanks to you!"

"The men will . . . talk!"

"I doubt it," the Earl replied. "I gave them the choice of being tried for attempted murder, which means at the very least transportation, or of disappearing and never being seen in the vicinity of my house again."

"You let them go?" Celesta asked incredulously.

"I did not want my future wife's name to be mentioned at any Trial."

Celesta gave a little sob.

"You tried to save the Wroxley honour but . . . you did not know . . . then about . . . Giles?"

"I did not know he was dead or that Crawthorne had killed him," the Earl answered, "but the two men they had employed told me what they were to be paid for murdering me."

Celesta put her hands up to her eyes.

"I am . . . ashamed!" she said in a low voice. "Ashamed that my brother should have behaved in such a . . . manner."

"No-one will ever know of it, and I am quite certain that it was all due to Crawthorne's bad influence when he encouraged your brother to drink until he could no longer think straight."

"That is . . . generous of you," Celesta murmured.

"All that people will know and talk about," the Earl went on, "is the fact that Giles tried to be free of Crawthorne and died in the process. There will be no Trial. There will be very little publicity, and I am quite certain that Crawthorne will save his skin even if it means crossing the Channel in a row-boat!"

There was a silence and then the Earl said softly:

"That just leaves you and me, Celesta!"

Celesta clasped her hands together.

"There is . . . something I want to . . . say to you."

"Could you not say it a little closer?" the Earl suggested.

She shook her head.

"No! It . . . is . . . difficult."

"I am listening," the Earl said quietly.

Celesta's elegant Parisian gown revealed the soft curves of her breasts, the smallness of her waist, and its colour made her skin seem dazzlingly white.

Looking at her the Earl thought he had never known a woman who was so unself-conscious of her beauty.

"When I came to dinner with . . . you at the Priory," Celesta began in a tremulous voice, "you suggested . . . something to me and I . . . refused you."

"If I remember correctly," the Earl replied, "you said you would rather die than accept such a proposition."

"I did not . . . understand . . . then," Celesta murmured.

"Understand what?"

"That you were . . . right about love. . . . It is . . . irresistible!"

"That is what I have found."

"Then . . . if you still . . . want me," Celesta went on, "I will come to . . . you because I am . . . afraid by myself . . . and because . . . because I want . . . so much to be with . . . you."

The Earl smiled.

"If you only knew, my darling, how much I have wanted to hear you say that," he answered. "But I also have some explaining to do and I find it very difficult to say what has to be said when we are so far apart."

He opened his arms and because she could not help it, Celesta went towards him.

It was like stepping back into Heaven, she thought, to feel him holding her; to know a sense of safety and security that she had never known before.

She raised her face and found his lips were very close to hers.

"I love you!" he said. "I love you more than I believed it was possible to love anyone!"

Celesta drew in her breath and waited for him to kiss her; but he did not do so.

"I want you!" the Earl said. "I want you until I can think of nothing except you. Your face is always before my eyes—you are with me every moment of the day—and I hold you in my arms all night!"

There was a depth to his voice that made her tremble, but she was not afraid.

She only knew that she vibrated to the desire in his tone and she felt again the flame flicker within her that had been awakened the last time he kissed her.

"I love you, Celesta!" the Earl said again. "I knew the first time we met that I had found something very wonderful that I have been seeking all my life."

His eyes searched her face before he went on:

"I had never before seen anyone so beautiful! I had never before felt an inexplicable magic which made me sure I must never lose you."

He felt a quiver run through her.

"We both knew instinctively we were a part of each other, my precious, but I told myself it was because

I was seeing you in the country without the competition of other women."

"Was that . . . why you asked me to your Ball?" Celesta asked.

"One reason," the Earl replied, "and another, somewhat hard to explain, is that I was using you, because at the precise moment you arrived at my house to tell me Giles was in prison, I saw how you could save me from what had become an intolerable situation."

Celesta knew he was speaking of Lady Imogen.

"I thought you . . . loved . . . her," she whispered.

"I already loved you completely and irrevocably," the Earl replied, "but I would not admit it to myself, would not acknowledge that my much-vaunted independence was at an end."

"I do not . . . wish you to feel tied."

"I am a very willing prisoner, my lovely darling, and I knew in my heart I was your captive the first moment we met."

"I thought I . . . hated you," Celesta murmured.

"Like you," the Earl said, "I did not understand about love—although I thought I did—so I offered you what I called 'my protection'!"

"That is what I . . . want!" Celesta murmured.

"And that is what you will always have," the Earl replied, "but what I suggested that night in the Library was, although I tried to pretend otherwise, an insult!"

His arms tightened.

"It was an insult not only to you, my darling, but also to our love, which we both knew was something so tremendous, so perfect, that there was no escape for either of us."

Because what he was saying thrilled her like quicksilver running through her body, Celesta turned her face against his shoulder and as she did so she drew closer to him.

She could hardly breathe as he went on:

"I had sworn never to marry, but that was only because I had never in my life met a woman whom I wanted as my wife until I met you. But, Celesta, when I kissed you for the second time it was so very different in every way to what a kiss had ever meant to me before."

His lips touched her hair.

"At Carlton House I found the King had been buying toys for another man's children. I knew then that I wanted to buy toys for my children—our children, my darling—yours and mine!"

Celesta gave a little sob. Then she looked up at him.

"It is because I love you so much . . . that I could not let our children be . . . touched by the . . . shadow of sin."

The Earl's eyes were on her face as she continued:

"Let me come to you. I would be . . . proud to be your . . . mistress . . . happy as long as I can be with you. But I would not want our children to suffer as I have suffered . . . or to hate as I have . . . hated."

"They will never do that!" the Earl said, his voice deep and positive.

He smiled down at her and she thought she had never seen a man look so happy.

"Firstly, my sweet life, because I would never let you leave me and there will be no other men in your life—that I can promise you! And secondly because if your mother's behaviour still disturbs you, I have something to show you."

He kissed her forehead before he released her to walk across the room and pick up from the floor where he had thrown it down with his hat a newspaper.

Celesta looked at him wonderingly as he came back to her holding *The Morning Post* in his hand.

"I bought this at Canterbury," he said. "There is something which concerns you on the front page."

He gave it into Celesta's hands and she looked down at the paragraph to which he pointed. It was headed:

THE MARCHIONESS OF HERON
We deeply regret to announce the death of the

Marchioness of Heron yesterday at a St. Al-
bans Nursing Home. The Marchioness was
thirty-nine and had been in ill-health for some
years. The Marquis of Heron, who is living
abroad, has been informed.

Celesta read it through, then looked up at the
Earl.

"I would not wish the new Marchioness of Heron,"
he said with a twist of his lips, "to be ashamed of her
daughter's behaviour."

Celesta gave a little laugh which was also a sob.
Then she was in his arms again and the newspaper
had fallen to the floor.

"Mama will be . . . happy!" she murmured.

"As we will be," the Earl answered. "There will be
no more fears, no more shadows."

"You are so important . . . you should not marry
someone of no consequence and . . . unknown to the
social world."

"You are the only person who is important to me,"
the Earl answered, "and the social world is already
acclaiming your beauty."

She looked up at him, a dawning radiance in her
eyes, her lips parted. He thought he had never believed a woman could look so lovely.

"You are . . . sure . . . you want me?"

"It will take me a life-time to tell you how much."

He pulled her crushingly against him so she could
hardly breathe.

"You are mine!" he said passionately, "every perfect
little part of you and I will teach you to love me as
I love you, until there is no longer any doubt in your
mind."

"There are no . . . doubts as to my . . . love."

"None?" he questioned.

"You fill the whole world . . . the sky and . . .
Heaven itself," she whispered. "I want only to . . .
belong to you . . . to be yours!"

Her voice was as passionate as his. Then because she was shy she hid her face again.

"My precious, my little love!" the Earl exclaimed.

Then he said softly:

"I suggest, my wonderful darling, that we waste no more time but find a Parson to marry us. After that my yacht is in the harbour and when the wind has abated we can set off to whatever country you most fancy for your honeymoon."

He paused to say with laughter in his voice:

"But as you insisted—I will be coming with you!"

Celesta looked up at him with tears in her eyes.

"Can we . . . really do . . . that?"

"I assure you that nothing and nobody is going to stop us," the Earl replied. "I love you, my precious, and I must have you alone."

"I, too, want to be . . . alone with . . . you," Celesta whispered.

His lips found hers.

For a moment they were gentle and she knew there was a dedication in his kiss.

Then as he felt her response, as the flame that had flickered into life the night before swept through them both and became a fire, Celesta found herself moving closer and still closer until she felt as if her whole body melted into his.

"I adore you! I worship you!" the Earl said hoarsely.

Celesta knew from the manner in which he spoke that he was offering her his heart and soul.

"I worship you . . . too!" she wanted to say but somehow words were impossible.

There was only the rapture and the over-whelming force of their love, which was irresistible.

ABOUT THE AUTHOR

BARBARA CARTLAND, the celebrated romantic author, historian, playwright, lecturer, political speaker and television personality, has now written over 150 books. Miss Cartland has had a number of historical books published and several biographical ones, including that of her brother, Major Ronald Cartland, who was the first Member of Parliament to be killed in the War. This book had a Foreword by Sir Winston Churchill.

In private life, Barbara Cartland, who is a Dame of the Order of St. John of Jerusalem, has fought for better conditions and salaries for Midwives and Nurses. As President of the Royal College of Midwives (Hertfordshire Branch), she has been invested with the first Badge of Office ever given in Great Britain, which was subscribed to by the Midwives themselves. She has also championed the cause for old people and founded the first Romany Gypsy Camp in the world.

Barbara Cartland is deeply interested in Vitamin Therapy and is President of the British National Association for Health.

Barbara Cartland

The world's bestselling author of romantic fiction. Her stories are always captivating tales of intrigue, adventure and love.

☐	THE TEARS OF LOVE	2148	$1.25
☐	THE BORED BRIDEGROOM	6381	$1.25
☐	JOURNEY TO PARADISE	6383	$1.25
☐	THE PENNILESS PEER	6387	$1.25
☐	NO DARKNESS FOR LOVE	6427	$1.25
☐	THE LITTLE ADVENTURE	6428	$1.25
☐	THE SHADOW OF SIN	6430	$1.25
☐	LESSONS IN LOVE	6431	$1.25
☐	THE DARING DECEPTION	6435	$1.25
☐	CASTLE OF FEAR	8103	$1.25
☐	THE GLITTERING LIGHTS	8104	$1.25
☐	A SWORD TO THE HEART	8105	$1.25
☐	THE KARMA OF LOVE	8106	$1.25
☐	THE MAGNIFICENT MARRIAGE	8166	$1.25
☐	THE RUTHLESS RAKE	8240	$1.25
☐	THE DANGEROUS DANDY	8280	$1.25
☐	THE WICKED MARQUIS	8467	$1.25
☐	THE FRIGHTENED BRIDE	8780	$1.25
☐	THE FLAME IS LOVE	8887	$1.25

Buy them at your local bookseller or use this handy coupon:

Bantam Book Catalog

It lists over a thousand money-saving best-sellers originally priced from $3.75 to $15.00 —bestsellers that are yours now for as little as 50¢ to $2.95!

The catalog gives you a great opportunity to build your own private library at huge savings!

So don't delay any longer—send us your name and address and 25¢ (to help defray postage and handling costs).